imagination

Someday, I hope I can draw the way Julia draws, imagining worlds that don't yet exist.

I know what most humans think. They think gorillas don't have imaginations. They think we don't remember our pasts or ponder our futures.

Come to think of it, I suppose they have a point. Mostly I think about what is, not what could be.

I've learned not to get my hopes up.

KATHERINE

The
ONE AND
ON

illustrations by
Patricia Castelao

APPLEGATE

LY Ivan

HARPER
An Imprint of HarperCollins*Publishers*

Library of Congress Cataloging-in-Publication Data

Applegate, Katherine.

The one and only Ivan / by Katherine Applegate.

    p.   cm.

Summary: When Ivan, a gorilla who has lived for years in a down-and-out circus-themed mall, meets Ruby, a baby elephant that has been added to the mall, he decides that he must find her a better life.

ISBN 978-0-06-199225-4 (trade bdg.) — ISBN 978-0-06-213579-7 (int. ed.) ISBN 978-0-06-301413-8 (trade bdg. movie tie-in) — ISBN 978-0-06-301414-5 (pbk movie tie-in) — IBN 978-0-06-301938-6 (paper-over-boards movie tie-in)

    [1. Gorilla—Fiction. 2. Elephants—Fiction. 3. Animals—Treatment—Fiction.] I. Patricia Castelao , ill. II. Title.

PZ7.A6483On 2011   2011010034

[Fic]—dc22   CIP

                                                             AC

Typography by Sarah Hoy

20 21 22 23 24   PC/LSCH   10 9 8 7 6 5 4 3 2 1

❖

First Edition

for Julia

*It is never too late to be
what you might have been.*
—attributed to George Eliot

glossary

chest beat: repeated slapping of the chest with one or both hands in order to generate a loud sound (sometimes used by gorillas as a threat display to intimidate an opponent)

domain: territory

the Grunt: snorting, piglike noise made by gorilla parents to express annoyance

me-ball: dried excrement thrown at observers

9,855 days (example): While gorillas in the wild typically gauge the passing of time based on seasons or food availability, Ivan has adopted a tally of days. (9,855 days is equal to twenty-seven years.)

Not-Tag: stuffed toy gorilla

silverback (also, less frequently, grayboss): an adult male over twelve years old with an area of silver hair on his back. The silverback is a figure of authority, responsible for protecting his family.

slimy chimp (slang; offensive): a human (refers to sweat on hairless skin)

vining: casual play (a reference to vine swinging)

I am Ivan. I am a gorilla.

It's not as easy as it looks.

names

People call me the Freeway Gorilla. The Ape at Exit 8. The One and Only Ivan, Mighty Silverback.

The names are mine, but they're not me. I am Ivan, just Ivan, only Ivan.

Humans waste words. They toss them like banana peels and leave them to rot.

Everyone knows the peels are the best part.

I suppose you think gorillas can't understand you. Of course, you also probably think we can't walk upright.

Try knuckle walking for an hour. You tell me: Which way is more fun?

patience

I've learned to understand human words over the years, but understanding human speech is not the same as understanding humans.

Humans speak too much. They chatter like chimps, crowding the world with their noise even when they have nothing to say.

It took me some time to recognize all those human sounds, to weave words into things. But I was patient.

Patient is a useful way to be when you're an ape.

Gorillas are as patient as stones. Humans, not so much.

how I look

I used to be a wild gorilla, and I still look the part.

I have a gorilla's shy gaze, a gorilla's sly smile. I wear a snowy saddle of fur, the uniform of a silverback. When the sun warms my back, I cast a gorilla's majestic shadow.

In my size humans see a test of themselves. They hear fighting words on the wind, when all I'm thinking is how the late-day sun reminds me of a ripe nectarine.

I'm mightier than any human, four hundred pounds of pure power. My body looks made for battle. My arms, outstretched, span taller than the tallest human.

My family tree spreads wide as well. I am a great ape, and you are a great ape, and so are chimpanzees and orangutans and bonobos, all of us distant and distrustful cousins.

I know this is troubling.

I too find it hard to believe there is a connection across time and space, linking me to a race of ill-mannered clowns.

Chimps. There's no excuse for them.

the exit 8 big top mall
and video arcade

I live in a human habitat called the Exit 8 Big Top Mall and Video Arcade. We are conveniently located off I-95, with shows at two, four, and seven, 365 days a year.

Mack says that when he answers the trilling telephone.

Mack works here at the mall. He is the boss.

I work here too. I am the gorilla.

At the Big Top Mall, a creaky-music carousel spins all day, and monkeys and parrots live amid the merchants. In the middle of the mall is a ring with benches where humans can sit on their rumps while they eat soft pretzels. The floor is covered with sawdust made of dead trees.

My domain is at one end of the ring. I live here because I am too much gorilla and not enough human.

Stella's domain is next to mine. Stella is an elephant. She and Bob, who is a dog, are my dearest friends.

At present, I do not have any gorilla friends.

My domain is made of thick glass and rusty metal and rough cement. Stella's domain is made of metal bars. The sun bears' domain is wood; the parrots' is wire mesh.

Three of my walls are glass. One of them is cracked, and a small piece, about the size of my hand, is missing from its bottom corner. I made the hole with a baseball bat Mack gave me for my sixth birthday. After that he took the bat away, but he let me keep the baseball that came with it.

A jungle scene is painted on one of my domain walls. It has a waterfall without water and flowers without scent and trees without roots. I didn't paint it, but I enjoy the way the shapes flow across my wall, even if it isn't much of a jungle.

I am lucky my domain has three windowed walls. I can see the whole mall and a bit of the world beyond: the frantic pinball machines, the pink billows of cotton candy, the vast and treeless parking lot.

Beyond the lot is a freeway where cars stampede without end. A giant sign at its edge beckons them to stop and rest like gazelles at a watering hole.

The sign is faded, the colors bleeding, but I know what it says. Mack read its words aloud one day: "COME TO THE EXIT 8 BIG TOP MALL AND VIDEO ARCADE, HOME OF THE ONE AND ONLY IVAN, MIGHTY SILVERBACK!"

Sadly, I cannot read, although I wish I could. Reading stories would make a fine way to fill my empty hours.

Once, however, I was able to enjoy a book left in my domain by one of my keepers.

It tasted like termite.

The freeway billboard has a drawing of Mack in his clown clothes and Stella on her hind legs and an angry animal with fierce eyes and unkempt hair.

That animal is supposed to be me, but the artist made a mistake. I am never angry.

Anger is precious. A silverback uses anger to maintain order and warn his troop of danger. When my father beat his chest, it was to say, *Beware, listen, I am in charge. I am angry to protect you, because that is what I was born to do.*

Here in my domain, there is no one to protect.

My neighbors here at the Big Top Mall know many tricks. They are an educated lot, more accomplished than I am.

One of my neighbors plays baseball, although she is a chicken. Another drives a fire truck, although he is a rabbit.

I used to have a neighbor, a sleek and thoughtful seal, who could balance a ball on her nose from dawn till dusk. Her voice was like the throaty bark of a dog chained outside on a cold night.

Children wished on pennies and tossed them into her plastic pool. They glowed on the bottom like flat copper stones.

The seal was hungry one day, or bored, perhaps, so she ate one hundred pennies.

Mack said she'd be fine.

He was mistaken.

Mack calls our show "The Littlest Big Top on Earth." Every day at two, four, and seven, humans fan themselves, drink sodas, applaud. Babies wail. Mack, dressed like a clown, pedals a tiny bike. A dog named Snickers rides on Stella's back. Stella sits on a stool.

It is a very sturdy stool.

I don't do any tricks. Mack says it's enough for me to be me.

Stella told me that some circuses move from town to town. They have humans who dangle on ropes twining from the tops of tents. They have grumbling lions with gleaming teeth and a snaking line of elephants, each clutching the limp tail in front of her. The elephants look far off into the distance so they won't see the humans who want to see them.

Our circus doesn't migrate. We sit where we are, like an old beast too tired to push on.

After our show, humans forage through the stores. A store is where humans buy things they need to survive. At the Big Top Mall, some stores sell new things, things like balloons and T-shirts and caps to cover the gleaming heads of humans. Some stores sell old things, things that smell dusty and damp and long forgotten.

All day, I watch humans scurry from store to store. They pass their green paper, dry as old leaves and smelling of a thousand hands, back and forth and back again.

They hunt frantically, stalking, pushing, grumbling. Then they leave, clutching bags filled with things—bright things, soft things, big things—but no matter how full the bags, they always come back for more.

Humans are clever indeed. They spin pink clouds you can eat. They build domains with flat waterfalls.

But they are lousy hunters.

gone

Some animals live privately, unwatched, but that is not my life.

My life is flashing lights and pointing fingers and uninvited visitors. Inches away, humans flatten their little hands against the wall of glass that separates us.

The glass says you are this and we are that and that is how it will always be.

Humans leave their fingerprints behind, sticky with candy, slick with sweat. Each night a weary man comes to wipe them away.

Sometimes I press my nose against the glass. My noseprint, like your fingerprint, is the first and last and only one.

The man wipes the glass and then I am gone.

artists

Here in my domain, I do not have much to do. You can only throw so many me-balls at humans before you get bored.

A me-ball is made by rolling up dung until it's the size of a small apple, then letting it dry. I always keep a few on hand.

For some reason, my visitors never seem to carry any.

In my domain, I have a tire swing, a baseball, a tiny plastic pool filled with dirty water, and even an old TV.

I have a stuffed toy gorilla, too. Julia, the daughter of the weary man who cleans the mall each night, gave it to me.

The gorilla has empty eyes and floppy limbs, but I

sleep with it every night. I call it Not-Tag.

Tag was my twin sister's name.

Julia is ten years old. She has hair like black glass and a wide, half-moon smile. She and I have a lot in common. We are both great apes, and we are both artists.

It was Julia who gave me my first crayon, a stubby blue one, slipped through the broken spot in my glass along with a folded piece of paper.

I knew what to do with it. I'd watched Julia draw. When I dragged the crayon across the paper, it left a trail in its wake like a slithering blue snake.

Julia's drawings are wild with color and movement. She draws things that aren't real: clouds that smile and cars that swim. She draws until her crayons break and her paper rips. Her pictures are like pieces of a dream.

I can't draw dreamy pictures. I never remember my dreams, although I sometimes awaken with my fists clenched and my heart hammering.

My drawings seem pale and timid next to Julia's. She draws the ideas in her head. I draw the things in my cage, simple items that fill my days: an apple core, a banana peel, a candy wrapper. (I often eat my subjects before I draw them.)

But even though I draw the same things over and over again, I never get bored with my art. When I'm drawing, that's all I think about. I don't think about where I am, about yesterday or tomorrow. I just move my crayons across the paper.

Humans don't always seem to recognize what I've drawn. They squint, cock their heads, murmur. I'll draw a banana, a perfectly lovely banana, and they'll say, "It's a yellow airplane!" or "It's a duck without wings!"

That's all right. I'm not drawing for them. I'm drawing for me.

Mack soon realized that people will pay for a picture made by a gorilla, even if they don't know what it is. Now I draw every day. My works sell for twenty dollars apiece (twenty-five with frame) at the gift shop near my domain.

If I get tired and need a break, I eat my crayons.

shapes in clouds

I think I've always been an artist.

Even as a baby, still clinging to my mother, I had an artist's eye. I saw shapes in the clouds, and sculptures in the tumbled stones at the bottom of a stream. I grabbed at colors—the crimson flower just out of reach, the ebony bird streaking past.

I don't remember much about my early life, but I do remember this: Whenever I got the chance, I would dip my fingers into cool mud and use my mother's back for a canvas.

She was a patient soul, my mother.

imagination

Someday, I hope I can draw the way Julia draws, imagining worlds that don't yet exist.

I know what most humans think. They think gorillas don't have imaginations. They think we don't remember our pasts or ponder our futures.

Come to think of it, I suppose they have a point. Mostly I think about what is, not what could be.

I've learned not to get my hopes up.

When the Big Top Mall was first built, it smelled of new paint and fresh hay, and humans came to visit from morning till night. They drifted past my domain like logs on a lazy river.

Lately, a day might go by without a single visitor. Mack says he's worried. He says I'm not cute anymore. He says, "Ivan, you've lost your magic, old guy. You used to be a hit."

It's true that some of my visitors don't linger the way they used to. They stare through the glass, they cluck their tongues, they frown while I watch my TV.

"He looks lonely," they say.

Not long ago, a little boy stood before my glass, tears streaming down his smooth red cheeks. "He must be the loneliest gorilla in the world," he said, clutching his mother's hand.

At times like that, I wish humans could understand me the way I can understand them.

It's not so bad, I wanted to tell the little boy. With enough time, you can get used to almost anything.

tv

My visitors are often surprised when they see the TV Mack put in my domain. They seem to find it odd, the sight of a gorilla staring at tiny humans in a box.

Sometimes I wonder, though: Isn't the way they stare at me, sitting in my tiny box, just as strange?

My TV is old. It doesn't always work, and sometimes days will go by before anyone remembers to turn it on.

I'll watch anything, but I'm particularly fond of cartoons, with their bright jungle colors. I especially enjoy it when someone slips on a banana peel.

Bob, my dog friend, loves TV almost as much as I do. He prefers to watch professional bowling and cat-food commercials.

Bob and I have seen many romance movies too. In a

romance there is much hugging and sometimes face licking.

I have yet to see a single romance starring a gorilla.

We also enjoy old Western movies. In a Western, someone always says, "This town ain't big enough for the both of us, Sheriff." In a Western, you can tell who the good guys are and who the bad guys are, and the good guys always win.

Bob says Westerns are nothing like real life.

the nature show

I have been in my domain for nine thousand eight hundred and fifty-five days.

Alone.

For a while, when I was young and foolish, I thought I was the last gorilla on earth.

I tried not to dwell on it. Still, it's hard to stay upbeat when you think there are no more of you.

Then one night, after I watched a movie about men in black hats with guns and feeble-minded horses, a different show came on.

It was not a cartoon, not a romance, not a Western.

I saw a lush forest. I heard birds murmuring. The grass moved. The trees rustled.

Then I saw him. He was a bit threadbare and scrawny, and not as good-looking as I am, to be honest. But sure enough, he was a gorilla.

As suddenly as he'd appeared, the gorilla vanished, and in his place was a scruffy white animal called, I learned, a polar bear, and then a chubby water creature called a manatee, and then another animal, and another.

All night I sat wondering about the gorilla I'd glimpsed. Where did he live? Would he ever come to visit? If there was a he somewhere, could there be a she as well?

Or was it just the two of us in all the world, trapped in our own separate boxes?

stella

Stella says she is sure I will see another real, live gorilla someday, and I believe her because she is even older than I am and has eyes like black stars and knows more than I will ever know.

Stella is a mountain. Next to her I am a rock, and Bob is a grain of sand.

Every night, when the stores close and the moon washes the world with milky light, Stella and I talk.

We don't have much in common, but we have enough. We are huge and alone, and we both love yogurt raisins.

Sometimes Stella tells stories of her childhood, of leafy canopies hidden by mist and the busy songs of flowing water. Unlike me, she recalls every detail of her past.

Stella loves the moon, with its untroubled smile. I love

the feel of the sun on my belly.

She says, "It is quite a belly, my friend," and I say, "Thank you, and so is yours."

We talk, but not too much. Elephants, like gorillas, do not waste words.

Stella used to perform in a large and famous circus, and she still does some of those tricks for our show. During one stunt, Stella stands on her hind legs while Snickers jumps on her head.

It's hard to stand on your hind legs when you weigh more than forty men.

If you are a circus elephant and you stand on your hind legs while a dog jumps on your head, you get a treat. If you do not, the claw-stick comes swinging.

Elephant hide is thick as bark on an ancient tree, but a claw-stick can pierce it like a leaf.

Once Stella saw a trainer hit a bull elephant with a claw-stick. A bull is like a silverback, noble, contained, calm like a cobra is calm. When the claw-stick caught in the bull's flesh, he tossed the trainer into the air with his tusk.

The man flew, Stella said, like an ugly bird. She never saw the bull again.

stella's trunk

Stella's trunk is a miracle. She can pick up a single peanut with elegant precision, tickle a passing mouse, tap the shoulder of a dozing keeper.

Her trunk is remarkable, but still it can't unlatch the door of her tumble-down domain.

Circling Stella's legs are long-ago scars from the chains she wore as a youth: her bracelets, she calls them. When she worked at the famous circus, Stella had to balance on a pedestal for her most difficult trick. One day, she fell off and injured her foot. When she went lame and lagged behind the other elephants, the circus sold her to Mack.

Stella's foot never healed completely. She limps when she walks, and sometimes her foot gets infected when she stands in one place for too long.

Last winter, Stella's foot swelled to twice its normal size. She had a fever, and she lay on the damp, cold floor of her domain for five days.

They were very long days.

Even now, I'm not sure she's completely better. She never complains, though, so it's hard to know.

At the Big Top Mall, no one bothers with iron shackles. A bristly rope tied to a bolt in the floor is all that's required.

"They think I'm too old to cause trouble," Stella says.

"Old age," she says, "is a powerful disguise."

a plan

It's been two days since anyone's come to visit. Mack is in a bad mood. He says we are losing money hand over fist. He says he is going to sell the whole lot of us.

When Thelma, a blue and yellow macaw, demands "Kiss me, big boy" for the third time in ten minutes, Mack throws a soda can at her. Thelma's wings are clipped so that she can't fly, but she still can hop. She leaps aside just in the nick of time. "Pucker up!" she says with a shrill whistle.

Mack stomps to his office and slams the door shut.

I wonder if my visitors have grown tired of me. Maybe if I learn a trick or two, it will help.

Humans do seem to enjoy watching me eat. Luckily, I am always hungry. I am a gifted eater.

A silverback must eat forty-five pounds of food a day if he wants to stay a silverback. Forty-five pounds of fruit and leaves and seeds and stems and bark and vines and rotten wood.

Also, I enjoy the occasional insect.

I am going to try to eat more. Maybe then we will get more visitors. Tomorrow I will eat fifty pounds of food. Maybe even fifty-five.

That should make Mack happy.

bob

I explain my plan to Bob.

"Ivan," he says, "trust me on this one: The problem is not your appetite." He hops onto my chest and licks my chin, checking for leftovers.

Bob is a stray, which means he does not have a permanent address. He is so speedy, so wily, that mall workers long ago gave up trying to catch him. Bob can sneak into cracks and crevices like a tracked rat. He lives well off the ends of hot dogs he pulls from the trash. For dessert, he laps up spilled lemonade and splattered ice cream cones.

I've tried to share my food with Bob, but he is a picky eater and says he prefers to hunt for himself.

Bob is tiny, wiry, and fast, like a barking squirrel. He is nut colored and big eared. His tail moves like weeds in the wind, spiraling, dancing.

Bob's tail makes me dizzy and confused. It has meanings within meanings, like human words. "I am sad," it says. "I am happy." It says, "Beware! I may be tiny, but my teeth are sharp."

Gorillas don't have any use for tails. Our feelings are uncomplicated. Our rumps are unadorned.

Bob used to have three brothers and two sisters. Humans tossed them out of a truck onto the freeway when they were a few weeks old. Bob rolled into a ditch.

The others did not.

His first night on the highway, Bob slept in the icy mud of the ditch. When he woke, he was so cold that his legs would not bend for an hour.

The next night, Bob slept under some dirty hay near the Big Top Mall garbage bins.

The following night, Bob found the spot in the corner of my domain where the glass is broken. I dreamed that I'd eaten a furry doughnut, and when I woke in the dark, I discovered a tiny puppy snoring on top of my belly.

It had been so long since I'd felt the comfort of another's warmth that I wasn't sure what to do. Not that I hadn't had visitors. Mack had been in my domain, of course, and many other keepers. I'd seen my share of rats zip past, and the occasional wayward sparrow had fluttered in through a hole in my ceiling.

But they never stayed long.

I didn't move all night, for fear of waking Bob.

wild

Once I asked Bob why he didn't want a home. Humans, I'd noticed, seem to be irrationally fond of dogs, and I could see why a puppy would be easier to cuddle with than, say, a gorilla.

"Everywhere is my home," Bob answered. "I am a wild beast, my friend: untamed and undaunted."

I told Bob he could work in the shows like Snickers, the poodle who rides Stella.

Bob said Snickers sleeps on a pink pillow in Mack's office. He said she eats foul-smelling meat from a can.

He made a face. His lips curled, revealing tiny needles of teeth.

"Poodles," he said, "are parasites."

picasso

Mack gives me a fresh crayon, a yellow one, and ten pieces of paper. "Time to earn your keep, Picasso," he mutters.

I wonder who this Picasso is. Does he have a tire swing like me? Does he ever eat his crayons?

I know I have lost my magic, so I try my very best. I clutch the crayon and think.

I scan my domain. What is yellow?

A banana.

I draw a banana. The paper tears, but only a little.

I lean back, and Mack picks up the drawing. "Another day, another scribble," he says. "One down, nine to go."

What else is yellow? I wonder, scanning my domain.

I draw another banana. And then I draw eight more.

three visitors

Three visitors are here: a woman, a boy, a girl.

I strut across my domain for them. I dangle from my tire swing. I eat three banana peels in a row.

The boy spits at my window. The girl throws a handful of pebbles.

Sometimes I'm glad the glass is there.

my visitors return

After the show, the spit-pebble children come back.

I display my impressive teeth. I splash in my filthy pool. I grunt and hoot. I eat and eat and eat some more.

The children pound their pathetic chests. They toss more pebbles.

"Slimy chimps," I mutter. I throw a me-ball at them.

Sometimes I wish the glass were not there.

sorry

I'm sorry I called those children slimy chimps.

My mother would be ashamed of me.

julia

Like the spit-pebble children, Julia is a child, but that, after all, is not her fault.

While her father, George, cleans the mall each night, Julia sits by my domain. She could sit anywhere she wants: by the carousel, in the empty food court, on the bleachers coated in sawdust. But I am not bragging when I say that she always chooses to sit with me.

I think it's because we both love to draw.

Sara, Julia's mother, used to help clean the mall. But when she got sick and grew pale and stooped, Sara stopped coming. Every night Julia offers to help George, and every night he says firmly, "Homework, Julia. The floors will just get dirty again."

Homework, I have discovered, involves a sharp pencil

and thick books and long sighs.

I enjoy chewing pencils. I am sure I would excel at homework.

Sometimes Julia dozes off, and sometimes she reads her books, but mostly she draws pictures and talks about her day.

I don't know why people talk to me, but they often do. Perhaps it's because they think I can't understand them.

Or perhaps it's because I can't talk back.

Julia likes science and art. She doesn't like Lila Burpee, who teases her because her clothes are old, and she does like Deshawn Williams, who teases her too, but in a nice way, and she would like to be a famous artist when she grows up.

Sometimes Julia draws me. I am an elegant fellow in

her pictures, with my silver back gleaming like moon on moss. I never look angry, the way I do on the fading billboard by the highway.

I always look a bit sad, though.

drawing bob

I love Julia's pictures of Bob.

She draws him flying across the page, a blur of feet and fur. She draws him motionless, peeking out from behind a trash can or the soft hill of my belly. Sometimes in her drawings, Julia gives Bob wings or a lion's mane. Once she gave him a tortoise shell.

But the best thing she ever gave him wasn't a drawing. Julia gave Bob his name.

For a long time no one knew what to call Bob. Now and then a mall worker would try to approach him with a tidbit. "Here, doggie," they'd call, holding out a French fry. "Come on, pooch," they'd say. "How about a little piece of sandwich?"

But he would always vanish into the shadows before anyone could get too close.

One afternoon, Julia decided to draw the little dog curled up in the corner of my domain. First she watched him for a long time, chewing on her thumbnail. I could tell she was looking at him the way an artist looks at the world when she's trying to understand it.

Finally she grabbed her pencil and set to work. When she was finished, she held up the page.

There he was, the tiny, big-eared dog. He was smart and cunning, but his gaze was wistful.

Under the picture were three bold, confident marks, circled in black. I was pretty certain it was a word, even though I couldn't read it.

Julia's father peered over her shoulder. "That's him exactly," he said, nodding. He pointed to the circled marks. "I didn't realize his name was Bob," he said.

"Me either," said Julia. She smiled. "I had to draw him first."

bob and julia

Bob will not let humans touch him. He says their scent upsets his digestion.

But every now and then I see him sitting at Julia's feet. Her fingers move gently, just behind his right ear.

Usually Mack leaves after the last show, but tonight he is in his office working late. When he's done, he stops by my domain and stares at me for a long time while he drinks from a brown bottle.

George joins him, broom in hand, and Mack says the things he always says: "How about that game last night?" and "Business has been slow, but it'll get better, you'll see," and "Don't forget to empty the trash."

Mack glances over at the picture Julia is drawing. "What're you making?" he asks.

"It's for my mom," Julia says. "It's a flying dog." She holds up her drawing, eyeing it critically. "She likes airplanes. And dogs."

"Hmm," Mack murmurs, sounding unconvinced. He looks at George. "How's the wife doing, anyway?"

"About the same," George says. "She has good days and bad days."

"Yeah, don't we all," Mack says.

Mack starts to leave, then pauses. He reaches into his pocket, pulls out a crumpled green bill, and presses it into George's hand.

"Here," Mack says with a shrug. "Buy the kid some more crayons."

Mack is already out the door before George can yell "Thanks!"

not sleepy

"Stella," I say after Julia and her father go home, "I can't sleep."

"Of course you can," she says. "You are the king of sleepers."

"Shh," Bob says from his perch on my belly. "I'm dreaming about chili fries."

"I'm tired," I say, "but I'm not sleepy."

"What are you tired of?" Stella asks.

I think for a while. It's hard to put into words. Gorillas are not complainers. We're dreamers, poets, philosophers, nap takers.

"I don't know exactly." I kick at my tire swing. "I think I may be a little tired of my domain."

"That's because it's a cage," Bob tells me.

Bob is not always tactful.

"I know," Stella says. "It's a very small domain."

"And you're a very big gorilla," Bob adds.

"Stella?" I ask.

"Yes?"

"I noticed you were limping more than usual today. Is your leg bothering you?"

"Just a little," Stella answers.

I sigh. Bob resettles. His ears flick. He drools a bit, but I don't mind. I'm used to it.

"Try eating something," Stella says. "That always makes you happy."

I eat an old, brown carrot. It doesn't help, but I don't tell Stella. She needs to sleep.

"You could try remembering a good day," Stella suggests. "That's what I do when I can't sleep."

Stella remembers every moment since she was born: every scent, every sunset, every slight, every victory.

"You know I can't remember much," I say.

"There's a difference," Stella says gently, "between 'can't remember' and 'won't remember.'"

"That's true," I admit. Not remembering can be difficult, but I've had a lot of time to work on it.

"Memories are precious," Stella adds. "They help tell us who we are. Try remembering all your keepers. You always liked Karl, the one with the harmonica."

Karl. Yes. I remember how he gave me a coconut when I was still a juvenile. It took me all day to open it.

I try to recall other keepers I have known—the humans who cleaned my domain and prepared my food and sometimes kept me company. There was Juan, who poured Pepsis into my waiting mouth, and Katrina, who used to poke me with a broom when I was sleeping, and Ellen, who sang "How Much Is That Monkey in the Window?" with a sad smile while she scrubbed my water bowl.

And there was Gerald, who once brought me a box of fat, sweet strawberries.

Gerald was my favorite keeper.

I haven't had a real keeper in a long time. Mack says he doesn't have the money to pay for an ape babysitter. These days, George cleans my cage and Mack is the one who feeds me.

When I think about all the people who have taken care of me, mostly it's Mack I recall, day in and day out, year after year after year. Mack, who bought me and raised me and says I'm no longer cute.

As if a silverback could ever be cute.

Moonlight falls on the frozen carousel, on the silent popcorn stand, on the stall of leather belts that smell like long-gone cows.

The heavy work of Stella's breathing sounds like the wind in trees, and I wait for sleep to find me.

the beetle

Mack gives me a new black crayon and a fresh pile of paper. It's time to work again.

I smell the crayon, roll it in my hands, press the sharp point against my palm.

There's nothing I love more than a new crayon.

I search my domain for something to draw. What is black?

An old banana peel would work, but I've eaten them all.

Not-Tag is brown. My little pool is blue. The yogurt raisin I'm saving for this afternoon is white, at least on the outside.

Something moves in the corner.

I have a visitor!

A shiny beetle has stopped by. Bugs often wander through my domain on their way to somewhere else.

"Hello, beetle," I say.

He freezes, silent. Bugs never want to chat.

The beetle's an attractive bug, with a body like a glossy nut. He's black as a starless night.

That's it! I'll draw *him*.

It's hard, making a picture of something new. I don't get the chance that often.

But I try. I look at the beetle, who's being kind enough not to move, then back at my paper. I draw his body, his legs, his little antennae, his sour expression.

I'm lucky. The beetle stays all day. Usually bugs don't linger when they visit. I'm beginning to wonder if he's feeling all right.

Bob, who's been known to munch on bugs from time to time, offers to eat him.

I tell Bob that won't be necessary.

I'm just finishing my last picture when Mack returns. George and Julia are with him.

Mack enters my domain and picks up a drawing. "What the heck is this?" he asks. "Beats me what Ivan thinks he's drawing. This is a picture of nothing. A big, black nothing."

Julia's standing just outside my domain. "Can I see?" she asks.

Mack holds my picture up to the window. Julia tilts her head. She squeezes one eye shut. Then she opens her eye and scans my domain.

"I know!" she exclaims. "It's a beetle! See that beetle

over there by Ivan's pool?"

"Man, I just sprayed this place for bugs." Mack walks over to the beetle and lifts his foot.

Before Mack can stomp, the beetle skitters away, disappearing through a crack in the wall.

Mack turns back to my drawings. "So you figure this is a beetle, huh? If you say so, kid."

"Oh, that's a beetle for sure," Julia says, smiling at me. "I know a beetle when I see one."

It's nice, I think, having a fellow artist around.

change

Stella is the first to notice the change, but soon we all feel it.

A new animal is coming to the Big Top Mall.

How do we know this? Because we listen, we watch, and most of all, we sniff the air.

Humans always smell odd when change is in the air.

Like rotten meat, with a hint of papaya.

guessing

Bob fears our new neighbor will be a giant cat with slitted eyes and a coiled tail. But Stella says a truck will arrive this afternoon carrying a baby elephant.

"How do you know?" I ask. I sample the air, but all I smell is caramel corn.

I love caramel corn.

"I can hear her," Stella says. "She's crying for her mother."

I listen. I hear the cars charging past. I hear the snore of the sun bears in their wire domain.

But I don't hear any elephants.

"You're just hoping," I say.

Stella closes her eyes. "No," she says softly, "not hoping. Not at all."

jambo

My TV is off, so while we wait for the new neighbor, I ask Stella to tell us a story.

Stella rubs her right front foot against the wall. Her foot is swollen again, an ugly deep red.

"If you're not feeling well, Stella," I say, "you could take a nap and tell us a story later."

"I'm fine," she says, and she carefully shifts her weight.

"Tell us the Jambo story," I say. It's a favorite of mine, but I don't think Bob has ever heard it.

Because she remembers everything, Stella knows many stories. I like colorful tales with black beginnings and stormy middles and cloudless blue-sky endings. But any story will do.

I'm not in a position to be picky.

"Once upon a time," Stella begins, "there was a human boy. He was visiting a gorilla family at a place called a zoo."

"What's a zoo?" Bob asks. He's a street-smart dog, but there's much he hasn't seen.

"A good zoo," Stella says, "is a large domain. A wild cage. A safe place to be. It has room to roam and humans who don't hurt." She pauses, considering her words. "A good zoo is how humans make amends."

Stella moves a bit, groaning softly. "The boy stood on a wall," she continues, "watching, pointing, but he lost his balance and fell into the wild cage."

"Humans are clumsy," I interrupt. "If only they would knuckle walk, they wouldn't topple so often."

Stella nods. "A good point, Ivan. In any case, the boy lay in a motionless heap, while the humans gasped and cried. The silverback, whose name was Jambo, examined the boy, as was his duty, while his troop watched from a safe distance.

"Jambo stroked the child gently. He smelled the boy's pain, and then he stood watch.

"When the boy awoke, his humans cried out, 'Stay still! Don't move!' because they were certain—humans are always certain about things—that Jambo would crush the boy's life from him.

"The boy moaned. The crowd waited, hushed, expecting the worst.

"Jambo led his troop away.

"Men came down on ropes and whisked the child to waiting arms."

"Was the boy all right?" Bob asks.

"He wasn't hurt," Stella says, "although I wouldn't be

surprised if his parents hugged him many times that night, in between their scoldings."

Bob, who has been chewing his tail, pauses, tilting his head. "Is that a true story?"

"I always tell the truth," Stella replies. "Although I sometimes confuse the facts."

lucky

I've heard the Jambo story many times. Stella says that humans found it odd that the huge silverback didn't kill the boy.

Why, I wonder, was that so surprising? The boy was young, scared, alone.

He was, after all, just another great ape.

Bob nudges me with his cold nose. "Ivan," he says, "why aren't you and Stella in a zoo?"

I look at Stella. She looks at me. She smiles sadly with her eyes, just a little, the way only elephants can do.

"Just lucky, I guess," she says.

arrival

The new neighbor arrives after the four-o'clock show.

When the truck comes lumbering toward the parking lot, Bob scampers over to inform us.

Bob always knows what's happening. He's a useful friend to have, especially when you can't leave your domain.

With a groan, Mack lifts the sliding metal door near the food court, the place where deliveries are made.

A big white truck is backing up to the door, belching smoke. When the driver opens the truck, I know that Stella is right.

A baby elephant is inside. I see her trunk, poking out from the blackness.

I'm glad for Stella. But when I glance at her, I see she is not glad at all.

"Stand back, everyone!" Mack yells. "We've got a new arrival. This is Ruby, folks. Six hundred pounds of fun to save our sorry butts. This gal is gonna sell us some tickets."

Mack and two men climb into the black cave of the

truck. We hear noise, scuffling, a word Mack uses when he's angry.

Ruby makes a noise too, like one of the little trumpets they sell at the gift store.

"Move," Mack says, but still there is no Ruby. "Move," he says again. "We haven't got all day."

Inside her domain, Stella paces as much as she's able: two steps one way, two steps the other. She slaps her trunk against rusty metal bars. She grumbles.

"Stella," I ask, "did you hear the baby?"

Stella mutters something under her breath, a word *she* uses when *she's* angry.

"Relax, Stella," I say. "It will be okay."

"Ivan," Stella says, "it will never, ever be okay," and I know enough to stop talking.

stella helps

The men are still yelling. Some of the yelling is at each other, but most of it is at Ruby.

We hear scrambling, pounding, shifting. The side of the truck shudders.

"I'm starting to like this elephant," Bob whispers.

"I'm getting the big one," Mack says. "Maybe she can coax the stupid brat out of the truck."

Mack opens Stella's door. "Come on, girl," he urges. He unties the rope attached to the floor bolt.

Stella pushes past Mack, nearly knocking him over. She rushes as best she can, limping heavily, toward the open back door of the truck. She catches her swollen foot on the edge of the ramp and winces. Blood trickles down.

Halfway up the ramp she pauses. The noise in the truck stops. Ruby falls silent.

Slowly Stella makes her way up the rest of the ramp. It groans under her weight, and I can tell how much she is hurting by the awkward way she moves.

At the top of the incline she stops. She pokes her trunk into the emptiness.

We wait.

The tiny gray trunk appears again. Shyly it reaches out, tasting the air. Stella curls her own trunk around the baby's. They make soft rumbling sounds.

We wait some more. A hush falls over the entire Big Top Mall.

Thud. Thud. Step, step, pause. Step, step, pause.

And there she is, so small she can fit underneath Stella with room to spare. Her skin sags, and she sways unsteadily as she makes her way down the ramp.

"Not the greatest specimen," Mack says, "but I got her cheap from this bankrupt circus out west. They had her shipped over from Africa. Only had her a month before they went bust." He gestures toward Ruby. "Thing is, people love babies. Baby elephants, baby gorillas, heck, give me a baby alligator and I could make a killing."

Stella ushers Ruby toward her domain. Mack and the two men follow. At Stella's door, Ruby hesitates.

Mack gives Ruby a shove, but she doesn't budge. "Doggone it, get a clue, Ruby," he mutters, but Ruby isn't moving, and neither is Stella.

Mack grabs a broom. He raises it. Instantly, Stella steps in front of Ruby to shield her.

"Get in the cage, both of you!" Mack shouts.

Stella stares at Mack, considering. Gently but firmly,

using her trunk, she nudges Ruby into her domain. Only then does Stella enter. Mack slams the door shut with a clang.

I see two trunks entwined. I hear Stella whispering.

"Poor kid," says Bob. "Welcome to the Exit 8 Big Top Mall and Video Arcade, Home of the One and Only Ivan."

old news

When Julia comes, she sits by Stella's domain and watches the new baby. She barely talks to me.

Stella doesn't talk to me either. She is too busy nuzzling Ruby.

She is cute, little Ruby, with her ears flapping like palm leaves, but I am handsome and strong.

Bob trots a circle around my belly before settling down in just the right spot. "Give it up, Ivan," he says. "You're old news."

Julia gets out a piece of paper and a pencil. I can see that she is drawing Ruby.

I move to the corner of my domain to pout. Bob grumbles. He doesn't like it when I disrupt his naps.

"Homework," Julia's father scolds. Julia sighs and puts her drawing aside.

I grunt, and Julia glances in my direction. "Poor old Ivan," she says. "I've been ignoring you, haven't I?"

I grunt again, a dignified, indifferent grunt.

Julia thinks for a moment, then smiles. She walks over to my domain, to the spot in the corner where the glass is broken. She slides papers through. She rolls a pencil across my cement floor.

"You can draw the baby elephant too," Julia says.

I bite the pencil in half with my magnificent teeth. Then I eat some paper.

tricks

Even after Julia and her father leave, I try to keep sulking. But it's no use.

Gorillas are not, by nature, pouters.

"Stella?" I call. "It's a full moon. Did you see?"

Sometimes, when we are lucky, we catch a glimpse of the moon through the skylight in the food court.

"I did," Stella says. She is whispering, and I realize that Ruby must be asleep.

"Is Ruby all right?" I ask.

"She's too thin, Ivan," Stella says. "Poor baby. She was in that truck for days. Mack bought her from a circus, the same way he bought me, but she hadn't been there long. She was born in the wild, like us."

"Will she be okay?" I ask.

Stella doesn't answer my question. "The circus trainers chained her to the floor, Ivan. All four feet. Twenty-three hours a day."

I puzzle over why this would be a good idea. I always try to give humans the benefit of the doubt.

"Why would they do that?" I finally ask.

"To break her spirit," Stella says. "So she could learn to balance on a pedestal. So she could stand on her hind legs. So a dog could jump on her back while she walked in mindless circles."

I hear her tired voice and think of all the tricks Stella has learned.

introductions

When I awake the next morning, I see a little trunk poking out between the bars of Stella's domain.

"Hello," says a small, clear voice. "I'm Ruby." She waves her trunk.

"Hello," I say. "I'm Ivan."

"Are you a monkey?" Ruby asks.

"Certainly not."

Bob's ears perk up, although his eyes stay closed. "He's a gorilla," he says. "And I am a dog of uncertain heritage."

"Why did the dog climb your tummy?" Ruby asks.

"Because it's there," Bob murmurs.

"Is Stella awake?" I ask.

"Aunt Stella's asleep," Ruby says. "Her foot is hurting, I think."

Ruby turns her head. Her eyes are like Stella's, black and long-lashed, bottomless lakes fringed by tall grass. "When is breakfast?" she asks.

"Soon," I say. "When the mall opens and the workers come."

"Where"—Ruby twists her head in the other direction—"where are the other elephants?"

"It's just you and Stella," I say, and for some reason, I feel we have let her down.

"Are there more of you?"

"Not," I say, "at the moment."

Ruby picks up a piece of hay and considers it. "Do you

have a mom and a dad?"

"Well . . . I used to."

"Everyone has parents," Bob explains. "It's unavoidable."

"Before the circus, I used to live with my mom and my aunts and my sisters and my cousins," Ruby says. She drops the hay, picks it up, twirls it. "They're dead."

I don't know what to say. I am not really enjoying this conversation, but I can see that Ruby isn't done talking. To be polite, I say, "I'm sorry to hear that, Ruby."

"Humans killed them," she says.

"Who else?" Bob asks, and we all fall silent.

All morning, Stella strokes Ruby, pats her, smells her. They flap their ears. They rumble and roar. They sway as if they're dancing. Ruby clings to Stella's tail. She slips under Stella's belly.

Sometimes they just lean into each other, their trunks twirled together like jungle vines.

Stella looks so happy. It's more fun to watch than any nature show I've ever seen on TV.

George and Mack are out by the highway. I can see them through one of my windows. They are next to each other on tall wooden ladders, leaning against the billboard that tells the cars to stop and visit the One and Only Ivan, Mighty Silverback.

George has a bucket and a long-handled broom. Mack has pieces of paper. He slaps one against the billboard. George dips the broom into the bucket. He wets the paper with the liquid from the bucket, and somehow the paper stays in place.

They put up many pieces before they are done.

When they climb down from the ladders, I see that they've added a picture of a little elephant to the billboard. The elephant has a lopsided smile. She is wearing a red hat, and her tail curls like a pig's. She doesn't look like Ruby.

She doesn't even look like an elephant.

I've only known Ruby one day, and I could have drawn her better.

art lesson

Ruby asks a lot of questions. She says, "Ivan, why is your tummy so big?" and "Have you ever seen a green giraffe?" and "Can you get me one of those pink clouds that the humans are eating?"

When Ruby asks, "What is that on your wall?" I explain that it's a jungle. She says the flowers have no scent and the waterfall has no water and the trees have no roots.

"I am aware of that," I say. "It's art. A picture made with paint."

"Do you know how to make art?" Ruby asks.

"Yes, I do," I say, and I puff up my chest, just a little. "I've always been an artist. I love drawing."

"Why do you love it?" Ruby asks.

I pause. I've never talked to anyone about this before. "When I'm drawing a picture, I feel . . . quiet inside."

Ruby frowns. "Quiet is boring."

"Not always."

Ruby scratches the back of her neck with her trunk. "What do you draw, anyway?"

"Bananas, mostly. Things in my domain. My drawings sell at the gift store for twenty-five dollars apiece, with a frame."

"What's a frame?" Ruby asks. "What's a dollar? What's a gift store?"

I close my eyes. "I'm a little sleepy, Ruby."

"Have you ever driven a truck?" Ruby asks.

I don't answer.

"Ivan?" Ruby asks. "Can Bob fly?"

A memory flashes past, surprising me. I think of my father, snoring peacefully under the sun while I try every trick I know to wake him.

Perhaps, I realize, he wasn't really such a sound sleeper after all.

treat

"How's that foot, old girl?" George asks Stella.

Stella pokes her trunk between the bars. She inspects George's right shirt pocket for the treat he brings her every night without fail.

George doesn't always bring me treats. Stella's his favorite, but I don't mind. She's my favorite too.

Stella sees that George's pocket is empty. She gives George a frustrated nudge with her trunk, and Julia giggles.

Stella moves to George's left pocket and discovers a carrot. Nimbly she removes it.

Mack walks past. "Toilet's plugged up in the men's bathroom," he says. "Big mess."

"I'll take care of it." George sighs.

Mack turns to leave. "Um, before you go, Mack," George says, "you might want to take a look at Stella's foot. I think it's infected again."

"Darn thing never does heal up right." Mack rubs his eyes. "I'll keep an eye on it. Money's tight, though. Can't be calling the vet every time she sneezes."

George strokes Stella's trunk. She inspects his pockets one more time, just in case.

"Sorry, girl," George says, as he watches Mack walk away.

elephant jokes

"Ivan? Bob?"

I blink. The dawn sky is a smudge of gray flecked with pink, like a picture drawn with two crayons. I can just make out Ruby in the shadows, waving hello with her trunk.

"Are you awake?" Ruby asks.

"We are now," says Bob.

"Aunt Stella's still asleep and I don't want to wake her 'cause she said her foot was hurting but I'm really, really"—Ruby pauses for a breath—"really bored."

Bob opens one eye. "You know what I do when I'm bored?"

"What?" Ruby asks eagerly.

Bob closes his eye. "I sleep."

"It's a little early, Ruby," I say.

"I'm used to getting up early." Ruby wraps her trunk around one of the bars on her door. "At my old circus we always got up when it was still dark and then we had breakfast and we walked in a circle. And then they chained my feet up, and that really hurt."

Ruby falls silent. Instantly Bob is snoring.

"Ivan?" Ruby asks. "Do you know any jokes? I especially like jokes about elephants."

"Um. Well, let me see. I heard Mack tell one once." I yawn. "Uhh . . . how can you tell that an elephant has been in the refrigerator?"

"How?"

"By the footprints in the butter."

Ruby doesn't react. I sit up on my elbows, trying not to disturb Bob. "Get it?"

"What's a refrigerator?" Ruby asks.

"It's a human thing, a cold box with a door. They put food inside."

"They put food in the door? Or food in the box? And is it a big box?" Ruby asks. "Or a little box?"

I can see this is going to take a while, so I sit up all the way. Bob slides off, grumbling.

I reach for my pencil, the one I snapped in half with my teeth. "Here," I say, "I'll draw you a picture of one."

In the dim light, it takes me a minute to find a piece of the paper Julia gave me. The page is a little damp and has a smear of something orange on it. I think it's from a tangerine.

I try my best to make a refrigerator. The broken pencil

is not cooperating, but I do what I can.

By the time I'm done, the first streaks of morning sun have appeared in flashy cartoon colors. I hold up my picture for Ruby to see.

She studies it intently, her head turned so that one black

eye is trained on my drawing. "Wow. You made that! Is this the thing you were telling me about before? Art?"

"Sure is. I can draw all kinds of things. I'm especially good at fruit."

"Could you draw a banana right now?" Ruby asks.

"Absolutely." I turn the paper over and sketch.

"Wow," Ruby says again in an awed voice when I hold up the page. "It looks good enough to eat!"

She makes a happy, lilting sound, an elephant laugh. It's like the song of a bird I recall from long ago, a tiny yellow bird with a voice like dancing water.

Strange. I'd forgotten all about that bird, how she'd wake me every morning at dawn, when I was still curled safely in my mother's nest.

It's a good feeling, making Ruby laugh, so I draw another picture, and another, along the edges of the paper: an orange, a candy bar, a carrot.

"What are you two up to?" Stella asks, moaning as she tries to move her sore foot.

"How are you this morning?" I ask.

"Just feeling my age," Stella says. "I'm fine."

"Ivan is making me pictures," Ruby says. "And he told me a joke. I really like Ivan, Aunt Stella."

Stella winks at me. "Me too," she says.

"Ivan? Want to hear my favorite joke?" Ruby asks. "I heard it from Maggie. She was one of the giraffes in my old circus."

"Sure," I say.

"It goes like this." Ruby clears her throat. "What do elephants have that nothing else has?"

Trunks, I think, but I don't answer because I don't want to ruin Ruby's fun.

"I don't know, Ruby," I reply. "What do elephants have that nothing else has?"

"Baby elephants," Ruby says.

"Good one, Ruby," I say, watching Stella stroke Ruby's back with her trunk.

"Good one," Stella says softly.

children

Once I asked Stella if she'd ever had any babies.

She shook her head. "I never had the opportunity."

"You would have made a great mother," I told her.

"Thank you, Ivan," Stella said, clearly pleased. "I like to think so. Having young ones is a big responsibility. You have to teach them how to take mud baths, of course, and emphasize the importance of fiber in their diet." She looked away, contemplating.

Elephants are excellent at contemplating.

"I think the hardest part of being a parent," Stella added after a while, "would be keeping your babies safe from harm. Protecting them."

"The way silverbacks do in the jungle," I said.

"Exactly." Stella nodded.

"You would have been good at protecting, too," I said confidently.

"I'm not so sure," Stella said, gazing at the iron bars surrounding her. "I'm not sure at all."

the parking lot

Mack and George are chatting while George cleans one of my windows.

"George," Mack says, frowning, "there's something wrong with the parking lot."

George sighs. "I'll take a look as soon as I'm done with this window. What's the problem?"

"There are cars in it, that's what's wrong. *Cars*, George!" Mack breaks into a grin. "I think things are actually starting to pick up a bit. It's gotta be the billboard. People see that baby elephant and they just have to stop and spend their hard-earned cash."

"I hope so," George says. "We sure could use the business."

Mack's right. I have noticed more visitors coming since

he and George added the picture of Ruby to the sign. People crowd around Ruby and Stella's domain, oohing and ahhing at the sight of a such a tiny elephant.

I gaze out at the huge sign that makes humans stop and spend their hard-earned cash. I have to admit that the picture of Ruby is rather cute, even if she doesn't look like a real elephant.

I wonder if Mack could add a little red hat and a curly tail to the picture of me. Maybe then more visitors would stop by my domain.

I could use a few oohs and ahhs myself.

"Ivan, tell me another joke, please!" Ruby begs after the two-o'clock show.

"I think I may have run out of jokes," I admit.

"A story, then," Ruby says. "Aunt Stella's sleeping. And there's nothing to do."

I tap my chin. I'm trying hard to think. But when I gaze up at the food court skylight, I'm mesmerized by the elephant-colored clouds galloping past.

Ruby taps her foot impatiently. "I know! *I'll* tell *you* a story," she says. "A real live true one."

"Good idea," I say. "What's it about?"

"It's about *me.*" Ruby lowers her voice. "It's about me and how I fell into a hole. A *big* hole. Humans dug it."

Bob pricks his ears and joins me by the window. "I always enjoy a good digging story," he says.

"It was a big hole full of water near a village," Ruby says. "I don't know why humans made it."

"Sometimes you just need to dig for the sake of digging," Bob reflects.

"We were looking for food," Ruby says, "my family and I. But I wandered off and got lost and went too close to the village." Ruby looks at me, eyes wide. "I was *so* scared when I fell into that hole."

"Of course you were," I say. "I would have been scared too."

"Me too," Bob admits. "And I *like* holes."

"The hole was huge." Ruby pokes her trunk between the bars and makes a circle in the air. "And guess what?" She doesn't wait for an answer. "The water was all the way up to my neck and I was sure I was going to die."

I shudder. "What happened then?" I ask.

"*I'll* tell you what happened," Bob says darkly. "They captured her and put her in a box and shipped her off and here she is. Just like they did with Stella." He pauses to scratch an ear. "Humans. Rats have bigger hearts. Roaches have kinder souls. Flies have—"

"No, Bob!" Ruby interrupts. "You're wrong. These humans helped me. When they saw I was trapped, they grabbed ropes and they made loops around my neck and my tummy. The whole entire village helped, even little kids and grandmas and grandpas, and they all pulled and pulled and . . ."

Ruby stops. Her lashes are wet, and I know she must be remembering all the terrible feelings from that day.

". . . and they saved me," she finishes in a whisper.

Bob blinks. "They *saved* you?" he repeats.

"When I was finally out, everyone cheered," Ruby

says. "And the children fed me fruit. And then all those humans led me back to my family. It took the whole day to find them."

"No way," Bob says, still doubtful.

"It's true," Ruby says. "Every word."

"Of course it's true," I say.

"I've heard rescue stories like that before." It's Stella's voice. She sounds weary. Slowly she makes her way over to Ruby. "Humans can surprise you sometimes. An unpredictable species, *Homo sapiens.*"

Bob still looks unconvinced. "But Ruby's here now," he points out. "If humans are so swell, who did that to her?"

I send Bob a grumpy look. Sometimes he doesn't know when to keep quiet.

Ruby swallows, and I'm afraid she's going to cry. But

when she speaks, her voice is strong. "Bad humans killed my family, and bad humans sent me here. But that day in the hole, it was humans who saved me." Ruby leans her head on Stella's shoulder. "Those humans were good."

"It doesn't make any sense," Bob says. "I just don't understand them. I never will."

"You're not alone," I say, and I turn my gaze back to the racing gray clouds.

a hit

Stella's foot hurts too much for her to do any hard tricks for the two-o'clock show. Instead, Mack pulls her, limping, into the ring, where she tracks a circle in the sawdust.

Ruby clings to her like a shadow. Ruby's eyes go wide when Snickers jumps on Stella's back, then leaps onto her head.

At the four-o'clock show, Stella can only get as far as the entrance to the ring. Ruby refuses to leave her side.

At the seven-o'clock show, Stella stays in her domain. When Mack comes for Ruby, Stella whispers something in her ear. Ruby looks at her pleadingly, but after a moment, she follows Mack to the ring.

Ruby stands alone. The bright lights make her blink. She flaps her ears. She makes her tiny trumpet sound.

The humans stop eating their popcorn. They coo.
They clap.

Ruby is a hit.

I don't know whether to be happy or sad.

worry

When Julia arrives after the show, she brings three thick books, one pencil, and something she calls Magic Markers.

"Here, Ivan," she says, and she slides two Magic Markers and a piece of paper into my domain.

I like the sundown colors, red and purple. But I don't feel like coloring. I'm worried about Stella. All evening she's been quiet, and she hasn't eaten a bit of her dinner.

Julia follows my gaze. "Where is Stella, anyway?" she asks, and she goes to Stella's gate. Ruby extends her trunk and Julia pats it. "Hi, baby," she says. "Is Stella all right?"

Stella is lying in a pile of dirty hay. Her breath is ragged.

"Dad," Julia calls, "could you come here a minute?"

George sets aside his mop.

"Do you think she's okay, Dad?" Julia asks. "Look at the way she's breathing. Can we call Mack? I think there's something really wrong."

"He must know about her." George rubs his chin. "He always knows. But a vet costs money, Jules."

"Please?" Julia's eyes are wet. "Call him, Dad."

George gazes at Stella. He puts his hands on his hips and sighs. He calls Mack.

I can't hear all of his words, but I can see George's lips tighten into a grim line.

Gorilla expressions and human expressions are a lot alike.

"Mack says the vet's coming in the morning if Stella's not any better," he tells Julia. "He says he's not going to let her die on him, not after all the money he's put into her."

George strokes Julia's hair. "She'll be all right. She's a tough old girl."

Julia sits by Stella's domain until it's time to go home. She doesn't do her homework. She doesn't even draw.

the promise

My domain gleams with moonlight when I awake to the sound of Stella's calls.

"Ivan?" Stella says in a hoarse whisper. "Ivan?"

"I'm here, Stella." I sit up abruptly, and Bob topples off my stomach. I run to a window. I can see Ruby next to Stella, sleeping soundly.

"Ivan, I want you to promise me something," Stella says.

"Anything," I say.

"I've never asked for a promise before, because promises are forever, and forever is an unusually long time. Especially when you're in a cage."

"Domain," I correct.

"Domain," she agrees.

I straighten to my full height. "I promise, Stella," I say in a voice like my father's.

"But you haven't even heard what I'm asking yet," she says, and she closes her eyes for a moment. Her great chest shudders.

"I promise anyway."

Stella doesn't say anything for a long time. "Never mind," she finally says. "I don't know what I was thinking. The pain is making me addled."

Ruby stirs. Her trunk moves, as if she is reaching for something that isn't there.

When I say the words, they surprise me. "You want me to take care of Ruby."

Stella nods, a small gesture that makes her wince. "If she could have a life that's . . . different from mine.

She needs a safe place, Ivan. Not—"

"Not here," I say.

It would be easier to promise to stop eating, to stop breathing, to stop being a gorilla.

"I promise, Stella," I say. "I promise it on my word as a silverback."

knowing

Before Mack, before Bob, even before Ruby, I know that Stella is gone.

I know it the way you know that summer is over and winter is on its way. I just know.

Stella once teased me that elephants are superior because they feel more joy and more grief than apes.

"Your gorilla hearts are made of ice, Ivan," she said, her eyes glittering. "Ours are made of fire."

Right now I would give all the yogurt raisins in all the world for a heart made of ice.

five men

Bob heard from a rat, a reliable sort, that they tossed Stella's body into a garbage truck.

It took five men and a forklift.

comfort

All day I try to comfort Ruby, but what can I say?

That Stella had a good and happy life? That she lived as she was meant to live? That she died with those who loved her most nearby?

At least the last is true.

crying

Julia cries all evening, while her father sweeps and mops and dusts and cleans the toilets.

When George sees Mack, he runs to him. I can only hear a few of his words. *Vet. Should have. Wrong.*

Mack shrugs. His shoulders droop. He leaves without a word.

When George wipes the fingerprints off my glass, his cheeks are wet. He doesn't meet my eyes.

When all the humans have left, I send Bob to check on Ruby. "How is she?" I ask when he returns.

"She was shivering," Bob says. "I tried to cover her with hay. And I told her not to worry, because you were going to save her."

I glare at him. "You *told* her that?"

"You promised Stella." Bob lowers his head. "I wanted to make the kid feel better."

"I shouldn't have made that promise, Bob. I just wanted—" I point to Stella's domain, and for a moment, it seems like I've forgotten how to breathe. "I wanted to make Stella happy, I guess. But I can't save Ruby. I can't even save myself."

I flop onto my back. The cement is always cold, but tonight it hurts.

Bob leaps onto my belly. "You are the One and Only Ivan," he says. "Mighty Silverback."

He licks my chin, and he's not even checking for leftovers.

"Say it," Bob commands.

I look away.

"Say it, Ivan."

I don't answer, so Bob licks my nose until I can't stand it any longer.

"I am the One and Only Ivan," I mutter.

"And don't you ever forget it," he says.

When I gaze at the food-court skylight, the moon Stella loved is shrouded in clouds.

All night, Ruby moans and sniffles. I pace my domain. I don't want to fall asleep, in case she needs something.

"Ivan," Bob says gently, "get some sleep. Please. For your sake. And for mine."

Bob can't sleep unless he is on my stomach.

I hear a stirring. "Ivan?" Ruby calls.

I rush to my window. "Ruby? Are you all right?"

"I miss Aunt Stella," Ruby sobs. "And I miss my mom and my sisters and my aunts and my cousins, too."

"I know," I say, because it's all I can think of.

Ruby sniffles. "I can't sleep. Do you know any stories

the way Aunt Stella did?"

"Not really," I admit. "Stories were Stella's specialty."

"Tell me a story about when you were little," Ruby pleads. She puts her trunk between the bars. "Please, Ivan?"

I scratch the back of my head. "I don't remember things, Ruby," I admit.

"It's true," Bob says, trying to be helpful. "Ivan has a terrible memory. He's the opposite of an elephant."

Ruby lets out a long, shivery breath. "Oh, well. That's okay. Night, Ivan. And Bob."

I listen to Ruby's soft sobs for long, horrible minutes.

Then I hear myself saying, "Once upon a time there was a gorilla named Ivan."

And, slowly and deliberately, I try to remember.

the grunt

I was born in a place humans call central Africa, in a dense rain forest so beautiful, no crayons could ever do it justice.

Gorillas don't name their newborns right away, the way humans do. We get to know our babies first. We wait to see hints of what might yet be.

When they saw how much she loved to chase me around the forest, my parents decided on my twin sister's name: Tag.

Oh, how I loved to play tag with my sister! She was nimble, but when I got too close, she would leap onto my unsuspecting father. Then I would join her and we would bounce on that tolerant belly until he gave us the Grunt, the rooting-pig sound that meant *Enough!*

That game never got old.

Although my father might have disagreed.

mud

It didn't take long for my parents to find my name. All day long, every day, I made pictures. I drew on rocks and bark and my poor mother's back.

I used the sap from leaves. I used the juice from fruit. But mostly I used mud.

And that is what they called me: Mud.

To a human, *Mud* might not sound like much. But to me, it was everything.

My family, which humans call a troop, was just like any other gorilla family. There were ten of us—my father, the silverback; my mother and three other adult females; a juvenile male called a blackback; and two other young gorillas. Tag and I were the babies of the group.

We squabbled now and then, as families will. But my father knew how to keep us in line with a simple scowl. And for the most part, we were happy to do what we were meant to do: to feed and forage and nap and play.

My father was a master at leading us to the ripest fruit for our morning feast and the finest branches for our night nests. He was everything a silverback is meant to be: a guide, a teacher, a protector.

And nobody could chest beat like my father.

a perfect life

Gorilla babies and elephant babies and human babies are not so different, except that a gorilla gets to spend the day riding on his mother's back, like a cowboy on a horse. It's a pretty great system, from the baby's point of view.

Slowly, carefully, a young gorilla begins to venture farther and farther away from the safety of his mother's arms. He learns the skills he will need as an adult. How to make a nest of branches (weave them tightly or they will fall apart in the middle of the night). How to beat your chest (cup your palms to amplify the sound). How to go vining from tree to tree (don't let go). How to be kind, be strong, be loyal.

Growing up gorilla is just like any other kind of growing up. You make mistakes. You play. You learn. You do it all over again.

It was, for a while, a perfect life.

the end

One day, a still day when the hot air hummed, the humans came.

vine

After they captured my sister and me, they put us in a cramped, dark crate that smelled of urine and fear.

Somehow I knew that in order to live, I had to let my old life die. But my sister could not let go of our home. It held her like a vine, stretching across the miles, comforting, strangling.

We were still in our crate when she looked at me without seeing, and I knew that the vine had finally snapped.

the temporary human

It was Mack who pried open that crate, Mack who bought me, and Mack who raised me like a human baby.

I wore diapers. I drank from a bottle. I slept in human beds, sat in human chairs, listened while human words swarmed around me like angry bees.

Mack had a wife back then. Helen was quick to laugh, but quick to anger, too, especially when I broke something, which was often.

Here is what I broke while I lived with Mack and Helen:

1 crib
46 glasses
7 lamps
1 couch

3 shower curtains
3 shower-curtain rods
1 blender
1 TV
1 radio
3 toes (my own)

I broke the blender when I squeezed three tubes of toothpaste and a bottle of glue into it. I broke my toes attempting to swing from a lamp fixture on the ceiling. I broke forty-six glasses . . . well, it turns out there are many ways to break a glass.

Every weekend, Mack and Helen took me in their convertible to a fast-food restaurant, where they ordered me French fries and a strawberry shake. Mack loved to see the expression on the cashier's face when he drove up and said, "Could I have some extra ketchup for my kid?"

I went to baseball games, to the grocery store, to a movie theater, even to the circus. (They didn't have a gorilla.) I rode a little motorbike and blew out candles on a birthday cake.

My life as a human was a glamorous one, although my parents, traditional sorts, would not have approved.

hunger

In my new life as a human, I was well tended. I ate lettuce leaves with Thousand Island dressing, and caramel apples, and popcorn with butter. My belly ballooned.

But hunger, like food, comes in many shapes and colors. At night, lying alone in my Pooh pajamas, I felt hungry for the skilled touch of a grooming friend, for the cheerful grunts of a play fight, for the easy safety of my nearby troop, foraging through shadows.

Remember what happened to Tag, I told myself. Don't think about the jungle.

Still, sometimes I lay awake, wishing for the warmth of another just like me, asleep in a night nest of tender prayer-plant leaves.

I liked having sips of soda poured into my mouth like a

bubbling waterfall. But every now and then, I longed to search for a tender stalk of arrowroot, to feel the tease of a mango, just out of reach.

still life

One day Helen came home with something large and flat, wrapped in brown paper.

"Look what I bought today," she said excitedly as she tore off the paper. "A painting to go over the living-room couch."

"Fruit in a bowl," Mack said with a shrug. "Big deal."

"This is fine art. It's called a 'still life,'" Helen explained. "And I think it's lovely."

I dashed over to examine the painting, marveling at the colors and shapes.

"See?" said Mack's wife. "Ivan likes it."

"Ivan likes to roll up poop and throw it at squirrels," Mack said.

I couldn't take my eyes off the apples and bananas and grapes in the picture. They looked so real, so inviting, so . . . edible.

I reached out to touch a grape, and Helen slapped my hand. "Bad boy, Ivan. Don't touch." She jerked her thumb at Mack. "Honey, go get a hammer and a nail, would ya?"

While Mack and Helen were busy in the living room, I wandered into the kitchen. A cake covered in thick chocolate frosting sat on the counter.

I like cake—love it, in fact—but it wasn't eating I was thinking about. It was painting.

The frosting peaked and dipped like waves on a tiny pond. It looked rich and gooey, dark and smooth.

It looked like mud.

I scooped up a handful of frosting. I scooped up another.

I headed to the refrigerator door. It was perfect: an empty, white, waiting canvas.

The frosting wasn't as easy to work with as jungle mud. It was stickier and, of course, more tempting to eat.

But I kept at it. I scraped off every last bit of that frosting.

I may have eaten a little cake, too.

I don't remember what I was trying to paint. A banana, most likely. I suppose I knew I was going to get in trouble.

But at that moment, I just didn't care. I wanted to make something, anything, the way I used to.

I wanted to be an artist again.

punishment

I soon learned that humans can screech even louder than monkeys.

After that, I was never allowed in the kitchen.

babies

Back in those days, the Big Top Mall was smaller. It had a pony ride, a wooden train that bustled around the parking lot, a few bedraggled parrots, and a surly spider monkey.

But when Mack brought me—a baby gorilla dressed in a crisp tuxedo—to the mall, everything changed.

People came from far and wide to have their pictures taken with me. They brought me blocks and a toy guitar. They held me in their laps. Once I even held a baby in mine.

She was small and slippery. Bubbles flowed from her lips. She squeezed my fingers. Her rear was puffy with padding. Her legs bowed like bent twigs.

I made a face. She made a face. I grunted. She grunted.

I was so afraid she would fall that I squeezed her tightly, and her mother yanked her away.

I wonder if my mother ever worried about dropping us. We always held on, but that's easier to do when your mother is furry.

Human babies are an ugly lot. But their eyes are like our babies' eyes.

Too big for their faces, and for the world.

beds

One day, after many weeks of loud talking, Helen packed a bag and slammed the front door and never came back.

I don't know why. I never know the why of humans.

That night, I slept with Mack in his bed.

My old nests were woven of leaves and sticks and shaped like his bathtub, cool green cocoons.

Mack's bed, like mine, was flat, hot, without sticks or stars.

Still, he made a sleeping sound like the rumble my father used to make when all was well, a sound from deep inside his belly.

my place

Mack grew sullen. I grew bigger. I became what I was meant to be, too large for chairs, too strong for hugs, too big for human life.

I tried to stay calm, to move with dignity. I did my best to eat daintily. But human ways are hard to learn, especially when you're not a human.

When I saw my new domain, I was thrilled, and who wouldn't have been? It had no furniture to break. No glasses to smash. No toilets to drop Mack's keys into.

It even had a tire swing.

I was relieved to have my own place.

Somehow, I didn't realize I'd be here quite so long.

Now I drink Pepsi, eat old apples, watch reruns on TV.

But many days I forget what I am supposed to be. Am I a human? Am I a gorilla?

Humans have so many words, more than they truly need.

Still, they have no name for what I am.

Ruby is finally asleep. I watch her chest rise and fall. Bob, too, is snoring.

But my mind is still racing. For perhaps the first time ever, I've been remembering.

It's an odd story to remember, I have to admit. My story has a strange shape: a stunted beginning, an endless middle.

I count all the days I've lived with humans. Gorillas count as well as anyone, although it's not a particularly useful skill to have in the wild.

I've forgotten so many things, and yet I always know precisely how many days I've been in my domain.

I take one of the Magic Markers Julia gave me. I make

an X, a small one, on my painted jungle wall.

I make more X's, and more. I make an X for every day of my life with humans.

My marks look like this: X X X X X X X.

The rest of the night, I mark the days, and when I am done, my wall looks like this:

And so on, until there are nine thousand eight hundred and seventy-six X's marching across my wall like a parade of ugly insects.

a visit

It's almost morning when I hear steps. It's Mack. He
has a sharp smell. He weaves as he walks.

He stands next to my domain. His eyes are red. He is
staring out the window at the empty parking lot.

"Ivan, my man," he mumbles. "Ivan." He presses his
forehead against the glass. "We've been through a lot,
you and me."

a new beginning

We don't see Mack for two days. When he returns, he doesn't talk about Stella.

Mack says he is anxious to teach Ruby some tricks. He says the billboard is bringing in more visitors. He says it's time for a new beginning.

All afternoon and into the evening Mack works with Ruby. Ruby's feet are looped with rope so that she cannot run. A heavy chain hangs off her neck. Mack shows her Stella's ball, her pedestal, her stool. He introduces her to Snickers.

When Ruby obeys Mack, he gives her a cube of sugar or a bit of dried apple. When she doesn't, he yells and kicks at the sawdust.

When George and Julia arrive, Mack is still training Ruby. Julia sits on a bench and watches them. She draws a little, but mostly she keeps her eyes on Ruby.

Bob watches too. He's hiding in the corner of my domain under Not-Tag. It's raining outside, and Bob does not like damp feet.

Ruby trudges behind Mack, her head drooping. Endlessly they circle the ring. Sometimes Mack slaps her flank with his hand.

Suddenly Ruby jerks to a stop. Mack pulls the chain hard, but Ruby refuses to move.

"Come on, Ruby." Mack is almost pleading. "What is your problem?"

"She's exhausted," I say to myself. "That's the problem."

Mack groans. "Idiot elephant."

"Idiot human," Bob mutters.

"Walk, Ruby," I say, although I know she's too far away

to hear me. "Do what he says."

"Walk," Mack commands. "Now."

Ruby doesn't walk. She plops her rump on the sawdust floor.

"I think maybe she's tired," Julia says.

Mack wipes his forehead with the back of his arm. "Yeah, I know. We're all tired."

He pushes Ruby with the heel of his boot. She ignores him.

George looks over from the food court, where he is wiping off tables. "Mack," he yells, "maybe you should call it a day. I'll close up."

Mack yanks on Ruby's chain. She's as anchored as a tree trunk. He pulls harder and falls to his knees. "That does it," Mack says. He brushes sawdust off his jeans. "I am through playing around."

Mack stomps off to his office. When he returns, he is carrying a long stick. The gleaming hook on its end is almost beautiful, like a sliver of moon.

It's a claw-stick.

Mack pokes Ruby with the sharp point. Not hard. Just a touch.

I can tell he wants her to see how much it can hurt.

I growl low in my throat.

Ruby doesn't budge. She is a gray, unmoving boulder. She closes her eyes, and for a moment I wonder if she might have fallen asleep.

"I'm warning you," Mack says. He breathes out. He stares at the ceiling.

Ruby makes a huffing sound.

"Fine," Mack says. "You want to play it that way?"

He draws back the claw-stick.

"No!" Julia cries.

"I'm not gonna hurt her," Mack says. "I just want to get her attention."

Bob snarls.

Mack swings. The hook slices the air just a few inches above Ruby's head.

"See why you don't want to mess with me?" Mack says. He draws back the claw-stick again. "Now *move!*"

Ruby jerks her head, flinging her trunk toward Mack.

She makes a noise that sends the sawdust scattering. It makes my glass shiver.

It is the most beautiful mad I have ever heard.

Ruby's trunk slaps into Mack.

I don't see exactly where she strikes him—somewhere below his stomach, I think—and I know he must be uncomfortable, because Mack drops the claw-stick and falls down on the ground and curls into a ball and howls like a baby.

"Direct hit," Bob says.

Mack groans. He stumbles to his feet and hobbles off toward his office. Ruby watches him leave. I can't read her expression. Is she afraid? Relieved? Proud?

When Mack is gone, George and Julia lead Ruby from the ring. "It's okay, baby, it's okay," Julia says, stroking Ruby's head.

They settle Ruby in her domain and make sure she has fresh water and food. Before long, Ruby's dozing.

"Dad?" Julia asks as George locks Ruby's iron door. "Do you think Mack would ever hurt Ruby?"

"I don't think so, Jules," George says. "At least I hope not."

"Maybe we could call someone."

George scratches his chin. "I wish I could help Ruby, but I wouldn't know how. I mean, who would I call? The elephant cops? Besides"—George looks down—"I need this job, Jules. *We* need this job. Your mom, the doctor bills . . ." He kisses the top of Julia's head. "Back to work. You and me both."

Julia sighs and reaches for her backpack. She removes a piece of paper, a bottle of water, and a small metal box.

"Homework first," George says, wagging a finger. "Then you can paint."

"It's for art class," Julia explains. "We're doing watercolors. I'm going to paint Ruby."

George smiles. "All right, then. Just don't forget your spelling."

"Dad?" Julia asks again. "Did you see Mack's face when Ruby hit him?"

George nods. "Yes," he says solemnly. "I did." He

shakes his head. "Poor Mack."

He turns away, and only then do I hear him laughing.

colors

Julia opens the metal box. I see a row of little squares. Green, blue, red, black, yellow, purple, orange: The colors seem to glow.

She pulls out a brush with a thin tuft of a tail at its end. She dips the brush in water and wets the paper, then taps at the red square.

When the brush meets the damp paper, pink petals of color unfurl like morning flowers.

I can't take my eyes off that magical brush. For a moment, I'm not thinking about Ruby and Mack and the claw-stick and Stella.

Almost.

Julia touches red again, then blue, and there, suddenly, is the purple of a ripe grape. She touches the blue, and her paper turns to summer sky. Black and white, and now I see that she is painting a picture of Ruby. I can make out her floppy ears, her thick legs.

Julia stops painting. She takes a few steps back, hands on her hips, gazing at her work.

She scowls. "It's not right," she says. She glances over her shoulder at me. I try to look encouraging.

Julia starts to crumple up the paper, then reconsiders. Instead she slides it into my cage at the spot where my glass is broken. "Here you go," she says. "A Julia original. That'll be worth millions someday."

Gingerly I pick up the paper. I do not eat a single bite of it.

"Oh. Hey, I almost forgot." Julia runs to her backpack. She pulls out three plastic jars—one yellow, one blue, one red.

She opens the jars, and an odd, not-food smell hits my nose. Julia pushes the jars, one by one, through the opening. Then she slides some paper through.

"These are called finger paints," she says. "My aunt gave them to me, but really, I'm too old for finger painting."

I stick a finger into the red jar. The paint is thick as mud. It's cool and smooth, like bananas underfoot.

I pop my finger into my mouth. It's not exactly ripe mango, but it's not bad.

Julia laughs. "You don't eat it. You paint with it." She grabs a piece of paper and presses her finger on it. "See? Like this."

I place my finger on a piece of paper. I lift it, and a red mark is there.

I get a bigger glob from the pot and slap my hand down

on the page. When I pull my hand off the paper, its red twin stays behind.

This isn't like the ghostly handprints on my glass, the ones my visitors leave behind.

This handprint can't be so easily wiped away.

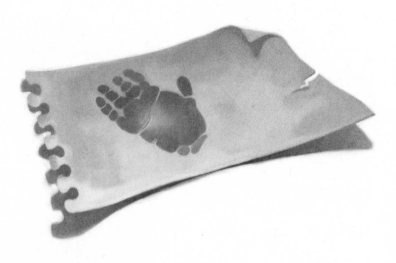

a bad dream

I lie awake, peeling dried red paint off my fingertips. Bob, who accidentally walked on one of my paintings, is licking his red paws.

Every so often, I glance over at the empty ring. The claw-stick glints in the moonlight.

"Stop! No!" Ruby's frantic cries startle me.

"Ruby," I call, "you're having a bad dream. You're okay. You're safe."

"Where's Stella?" she asks, gulping air. Before I can answer, she says, "Never mind. I remember now."

"Go back to sleep, Ruby," I say. "You've had a hard day."

"I can't go back to sleep," she says. "I'm afraid I'll

have the same dream. There was a sharp stick, and it hurt. . . ."

I look at Bob, and he looks back at me.

"Oh," Ruby says. "Oh. Mack." She puts her trunk between the bars. "Do you think—" She hesitates. "Do you think Mack is mad because I hurt him today?"

I consider lying, but gorillas are terrible liars. "Probably," I finally say.

"He ran away after that," Ruby says.

Bob gives a scornful laugh. "Crawled away is more like it."

We are quiet for a while. Branches claw at the roof. A light rain drums. One of the parrots murmurs something in her sleep.

Ruby breaks the silence. "Ivan? I smell something funny."

"He can't help it," Bob says.

"I believe she's referring to the finger paints Julia gave me," I say.

"What are finger paints?" Ruby asks.

"You make pictures with them," I explain.

"Could you make a picture of me?"

"Maybe someday." I remember Julia's picture, the one that will be worth a million dollars. I hold it up to the glass. "Look. It's you. Julia made it."

"It's hard to see," Ruby says. "There's not much moonlight. Why do I have two trunks?"

I examine the picture. "Those are feet."

"Why do I have two feet?"

"That's called artistic license," Bob says.

163

Ruby sighs. "Could you tell me another story?" she asks. "I don't think I can ever go back to sleep."

"I told you all I remember," I say with a helpless shrug.

"Then tell me a new story," she says. "Make something up."

I try to think, but my thoughts keep returning to Mack and his claw-stick.

"Anything yet?" Ruby asks.

"I'm working on it."

"Ivan?" Ruby presses. "Bob said you are going to save me."

"I . . ." I search for true words. "I'm working on that, too."

"Ivan?" Ruby says in a voice so low I can barely hear her. "I have another question."

I can tell from the sound of her voice that this will be a question I don't want to answer.

Ruby taps her trunk against the rusty iron bars of her door. "Do you think," she asks, "that I'll die in this domain someday, like Aunt Stella?"

Once again I consider lying, but when I look at Ruby, the half-formed words die in my throat. "Not if I can help it," I say instead.

I feel something tighten in my chest, something dark and hot. "And it's not a domain," I add.

I pause, and then I say it. "It's a cage."

I look at the ring, layered with fresh sawdust. I look at the skylight, at the half-hidden moon.

"I just thought of a story," I say.

"Is it a made-up story or a true one?" Ruby asks.

"True," I say. "I hope."

Ruby leans against the bars. Her eyes hold the pale moon in them, the way a still pond holds stars.

"Once upon a time," I say, "there was a baby elephant. She was smart and brave, and she needed to go to a place called a zoo."

"What's a zoo?" Ruby asks.

"A zoo, Ruby, is a place where humans make amends.

A good zoo is a place where humans care for animals and keep them safe."

"Did the baby elephant get to the zoo?" Ruby asks softly.

I don't answer right away. "Yes," I say at last.

"How did she get there?" Ruby asks.

"She had a friend," I say. "A friend who made a promise."

how

It takes a long time, but finally Ruby returns to sleep.

"Ivan," Bob whispers, yawning, "what you said . . . about the zoo. How are you going to do it?"

Suddenly I feel as if I could sleep for a thousand days. "I don't know," I admit.

"You'll think of something," Bob says confidently, his voice trailing off as his eyes close.

"What if I don't?" I ask, but Bob is already asleep.

His little red feet dance, and I know he's running in his dreams.

remembering

Bob and Ruby sleep on.

I don't sleep. I think about the promise I made to Stella, and the pictures I've made for Ruby. And I remember.

I remember it all.

what they did

We were clinging to our mother, my sister and I, when the humans killed her.

They shot my father next.

Then they chopped off their hands, their feet, their heads.

something else to buy

There is a cluttered, musty store near my cage.

They sell an ashtray there. It is made from the hand of
a gorilla.

another ivan

When morning comes and the parking lot glimmers
with dew, I see the billboard on the highway.

There I am: the One and Only Ivan, bathed in the pink
light of dawn. I look so angry, with my furrowed brow
and clenched fists.

I look the way my father did, the day the men came.

I am, I suppose, a peaceful sort. Mostly I watch the
world go by and think about naps and bananas and
yogurt raisins.

But inside me, hidden, is another Ivan.

He could tear a grown man's limbs off his body.

In the flicker of time it takes a snake's tongue to taste
the air, he could taste revenge.

He is the Ivan on the billboard.

I stare at the One and Only Ivan, at the faded picture of Stella, and I remember George and Mack on their ladders, adding the picture of Ruby to bring new visitors to the Exit 8 Big Top Mall and Video Arcade.

I remember the story Ruby told, the one where the villagers came to her rescue.

I hear Stella's kind, wise voice: *Humans can surprise you sometimes.*

I look at my fingers, coated in red paint the color of blood, and I know how to keep my promise.

days

During the days, I wait. During the nights, I paint.

I worry when Mack takes Ruby into the ring.

He carries the claw-stick with him all the time now.
He doesn't use it. He doesn't have to.

Ruby isn't fighting back anymore. She does whatever
Mack asks.

nights

I close my eyes. I dip my fingers into the paint.

When I'm done with one piece of paper, I set it aside to dry.

It's so small, just one sheet. And I'm going to need so many.

I move on to the next, and the next, and the next.

It's a giant puzzle, and I'm making the pieces one by one.

By morning, my floor is covered with paintings.

I hide the paintings under my pool of dirty water before Mack can see them. I don't want them to end up in the gift store, selling for twenty dollars apiece (twenty-five with frame).

These paintings are for Ruby. Every one of them.

"Ivan," Ruby asks one morning when I am trying to nap, "why are you always so sleepy during the day?"

"I've been working on a project at night," I tell her.

"What's a project?"

"It's . . . a thing. A painting. It's a painting for you, actually," I answer.

Ruby looks pleased. "Can I see it?"

"Not yet."

Ruby pokes with annoyance at her roped foot. She takes a breath. "Ivan? Do I have to do the shows with Mack today?"

"I'm afraid so. I'm sorry, Ruby."

Ruby dips her trunk in her water bucket. "That's okay," she says. "I already knew the answer."

not right

It's night again, and everyone's asleep. I look at the picture I've just made, one of dozens.

It's smudged and torn, a muddy blur.

I place it beside the others lining my floor.

The colors are wrong. The shapes are off. It looks like nothing.

It's not what I'm trying to create. It's not what it's meant to be.

It's not right, and I don't know why.

Across the parking lot the billboard beckons, as it always does: COME TO THE EXIT 8 BIG TOP MALL AND VIDEO ARCADE, HOME OF THE ONE AND ONLY IVAN, MIGHTY SILVERBACK!

If I could use human words to say what I need to say, this would all be so easy.

Instead, I have my pots of paint and my ragged pages.

I sigh. My fingertips glow like jungle flowers.

I try again.

going nowhere

I watch Ruby plod around the ring in endless circles, going nowhere.

More visitors have been coming, but not many. Mack says Ruby's not picking up the slack after all. He says he's cutting back on our food. He says he's turning off the heat at night to save money.

Ruby looks thinner to me, more wrinkled than Stella ever was.

"Do you think Ruby's eating enough?" I ask Bob.

"I don't know. I'll tell you one thing, though: You're sure as heck painting enough." Bob wrinkles his nose. "That stench is unbelievable. And I found yellow paint in my tail this morning."

Bob isn't happy about my night painting. He says it's unnatural.

Now, while I work at my art, Bob sleeps on Not-Tag. He claims he prefers her because she doesn't snore. He says her belly doesn't rise and fall and make him seasick.

"What is this plan of yours, anyway?" Bob asks. "If you explained it to me, I could help out." He gnaws at his tail. "Maybe I could come up with something that doesn't involve . . . you know, paint."

"I can't explain it," I tell him. "It's an idea in my head, but I can't get it right. And anyway, I'm almost out of supplies. I should have known I wouldn't have enough." I kick at my tire swing. It's spattered with drops of blue paint. "It's a stupid idea."

"I doubt that," Bob says. "Smelly, yes. Stupid? Never."

bad guys

Most of the day I doze. Late in the afternoon, Mack approaches.

Bob slips under Not-Tag. He prefers to keep a low profile around Mack.

Mack's gaze falls on my pool. A corner of one of my paintings is visible. "What's that, big guy?" he asks.

I calmly eat an orange, ignoring him, but my heart is racing.

Mack kicks at my plastic pool. Underneath it are all the paintings.

Mack yanks on a piece of paper. It slips out easily, and he doesn't seem to notice the other paintings.

The page is striped with green, which is what happens

when blue paint and yellow paint get together. It's supposed to be a patch of grass.

"Not bad. Where'd you get the paint, anyway? George's kid?" He considers. "Hmm. I'll bet I can get thirty for this picture, maybe even forty."

Mack turns on my TV. It's a Western. There's a human with a big hat and a small gun. He has a shiny star pinned to his chest. That means he is the sheriff and he will be getting rid of all the bad guys.

"If this sells quick, I'm getting you some more of that paint, buddy," Mack says.

He walks away with my painting. Ruby's painting. For a moment, I imagine what it would feel like to be the sheriff.

ad

"Good news, huh?" Bob says when Mack's out of earshot. "Looks like you might be getting some more supplies."

"I don't want to paint for Mack," I say. "I'm painting for Ruby."

"You can do both," Bob says. "You're an artist, after all."

While I watch the movie, I try to come up with a new hiding place for my paintings. Maybe, I think, I could fold them, once they're dry, and stuff them into Not-Tag.

It's a long movie. At the end, the sheriff marries the woman who owns the saloon, which is a watering hole for humans but not horses.

It's been a long time since I've seen a Western that was also a romance.

"I liked that movie," I say to Bob.

"Too many horses, not enough dogs," he comments.

An ad comes on.

I don't understand ads. They're not like Westerns, where you know who the bad guy is supposed to be. And they're hardly ever romantic, unless the man and the woman are brushing their teeth before they face lick.

I watch an ad for underarm deodorant. "How do you know who's who if they don't smell?" I ask Bob.

"Humans reek," Bob replies. "They just don't notice because they have incompetent noses."

Another ad comes on. I see children and their parents buying tickets, just like the tickets Mack sells. They laugh, enjoying their ice cream cones as they walk down a path.

They pause to watch two sleepy-eyed cats, huge and

striped, dozing in long grass.

Tigers. I know, because I saw them on a nature show once.

Words flash on the screen, accompanied by a drawing of a red giraffe. The giraffe vanishes, and I see a human family staring at another kind of family. Elephants, old and young. They're surrounded by rocks and trees and grass and room to wander.

It's a wild cage. A zoo. I see where it begins, and where it ends, the wall that says you are this and we are that and that is how it will always be.

It's not a perfect place. Even in just a few fleeting seconds on my TV screen, I can see that. A perfect place would not need walls.

But it's the place I need.

I gaze at the elephants, and then I look over at Ruby, small and alone.

Before the ad ends, I try to remember every last detail. Rocks, trees, tails, trunks.

It's the picture I need to paint.

imagining

It's different now, when I paint.

I'm not painting what I see in front of me. A banana.
An apple. I'm painting what I see in my head. Things
that don't exist.

At least, not yet.

not-tag

I pull out Not-Tag's stuffing. Carefully I fill her with my paintings, hiding them so Mack won't sell them. She's large, bigger than Bob, but I still have to crumple a few of them.

Bob tries to settle on her for a nap. "You've killed her," he complains.

"I had to," I say.

"I miss your stomach," Bob admits. "It's so . . . spacious."

When Julia arrives, she notices that I've used up my paints and paper. "Wow." Julia shakes her head. "You are one serious artist, Ivan."

one more thing

My finger painting has sold for forty dollars (with frame). Mack is happy. He brings me a huge pile of paper and big buckets of paint.

"Get to work," he says.

I paint for Mack during the day, and for Ruby at night.

I nap when I can.

But my nighttime picture isn't quite right. It's big, that's for sure. When I place all the pieces on the floor of my cage side by side, the cement is almost completely covered.

But something is still missing.

Bob says I'm crazy. "There's Ruby," he says, pointing with his nose. "There's the zoo. There are other elephants. What's wrong with it?"

"It needs one more thing," I say.

Bob groans. "You're being a temperamental artist. What could be missing?"

I stare at the huge expanse of colors and shapes. I don't know how to explain to Bob that it isn't done yet.

"I'll just have to wait," I say at last. "Something will come to me, and then I'll know my painting is finally ready."

the seven-o'clock show

During the last show of the day, Ruby seems tired.
When she stumbles, Mack reaches for the claw-stick.

I tense, waiting for her to strike back.

Ruby doesn't even flinch. She just keeps plodding
along, and after a while, Snickers jumps onto her back.

twelve

I lie in my cage, with Bob on my stomach. We are watching Julia do her homework.

She doesn't seem to be enjoying it. I can tell because she is sighing more than usual.

Again, for the hundredth time, or maybe the thousandth, I wonder what is missing from my painting.

And for the hundredth time, or maybe the thousandth, I don't have any answer.

"Dad," Julia says as George passes by with a mop, "can I ask you a question?"

"*May* I," George corrects. "Ask away."

Julia glances down at a piece of paper. "What's the difference between the word spelled P-R-I-N-C-I-P-A-L and the one spelled P-R-I-N-C-I-P-L-E?"

"The first one is the head of a school, like Ms. Garcia. The second one is a belief that helps you know what's right or wrong." He smiles. "For example, it's against my principles to do my daughter's homework for her."

Julia groans. "If I'm going to be an artist when I grow up, why do I need to know how to spell?"

With a laugh, George heads off.

Poor Julia, I think. Gorillas get by just fine without learning how to spell. All those endless letters, those sticks and circles and zigzags, filling up books and magazines, billboards and candy wrappers.

Words.

Humans love their words.

I leap up. Bob goes flying, straight into my pool.

A word.

"You know how I feel about wet feet!" Bob yells. He scrambles out of the water, shaking each foot in dismay.

I look out my window at the billboard. I can still hear Mack's voice in my head: "COME TO THE EXIT 8 BIG TOP MALL AND VIDEO ARCADE, HOME OF THE ONE AND ONLY IVAN, MIGHTY SILVERBACK!"

I count to twelve, and then I count again, just to be sure.

H

I lay out sixteen pieces of poster board. Four down, four across.

A perfect square.

"What are you up to?" Bob demands. "I'm guessing it doesn't involve sleep."

"It has to do with the billboard."

"That sign's a monstrosity. Particularly since I'm not featured."

I grab my bucket of red paint. "You're not on the billboard because you're not in the show," I point out.

"Technically, I don't even live here," Bob says with a sniff. "I am homeless by choice."

"I know. I'm just saying."

I study the billboard. Then I make two fat lines, like broom handles. Another fat line connects them.

I stand back. "What do you think?"

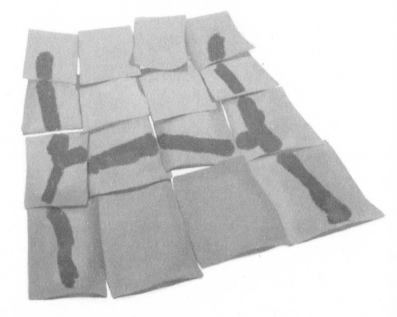

"What is it? No, wait: let me guess. A ladder?"

"Not a ladder," I say. "A *letter*. At least I think that's what they're called. I have to make three more."

Bob cuddles up next to Not-Tag. "Why?" he asks, yawning.

"Because then I'll have a word. A very important word." I dip my fingers into the paint.

"What word?" Bob asks.

"Home."

Bob closes his eyes. "That's not so important," he says quietly.

All day long I knuckle walk circles around my cage.

I'm so nervous I can't nap. I can't even eat.

Well, not very much, anyway.

I'm ready to show Julia what I've made.

It has to be Julia. She's an artist. Surely she'll look, truly look, at my painting. She won't notice the smudges and tears. She won't care if the pieces don't quite fit together. She'll see past all of that.

Surely Julia will see what I've imagined.

I watch Ruby trudge sullenly through the four-o'clock show, and I wonder: What will happen if I fail? What if I can't make Julia understand?

But of course I know the answer. Nothing. Nothing will happen.

Ruby will remain the main attraction at the Exit 8 Big Top Mall and Video Arcade, conveniently located off I-95, with shows at two, four, and seven, 365 days a year, year after year after year.

showing julia

It's time to show my work.

The mall is silent, except for Thelma the macaw, who is practicing a new phrase: "Uh-oh!"

Julia is finishing her homework. George is sweeping outside. Mack has gone home for the night.

I grab Not-Tag and carefully pull out the folded papers. So many paintings! Page after page. Piece after piece of my giant puzzle.

I pound on my glass, and Julia glances over.

Fingers trembling, I hold up one of my paintings. It's brown and green, a corner piece.

Julia smiles.

I display another picture, and then another and another and another, each one a tiny part of the whole.

Julia looks confused. "But . . . what is it?" she asks. She shrugs. "It doesn't matter. It's pretty just as it is."

"Uh-oh," says Thelma.

No, I think. *No.*

It does matter.

more paintings

George calls out to Julia. He's done for the night. "Grab your backpack," he says. "And hurry. It's late."

"Gotta go, Ivan," Julia says.

Julia doesn't understand.

I have to find the right pieces. I dig through the pile. They're here somewhere. I know they are.

I find one, another one, another. I try to hold four of them up against the glass.

"Bob," I say, "help me. Hurry!"

Bob grabs paintings with his teeth and drags them to me.

One by one, I shove pictures through the window crack. They crumple and tear.

There are too many pieces. My puzzle is too big.

"Careful, Ivan," Julia says. "Those might be worth millions someday. You never know." She arranges the paintings into a neat stack. "I suppose Mack's going to want to sell these in the gift shop."

She still doesn't understand.

I shove more out the hole and more and more, all of them, one after another.

"So Ivan's been painting, has he?" George says as he puts on his coat.

"A lot," says Julia with a laugh. "A *whole* lot."

"You're not taking all those home with you, are you?" George asks. "I mean, no offense to Ivan, but they're just blobs."

Julia thumbs through the towering stack of paintings. "They might not be blobs to Ivan."

"Let's leave those by the office," George suggests. "Mack'll want to try selling them. Although why anyone would pay forty bucks for a finger painting a two-year-old could do, I don't know."

"*I* like Ivan's work," Julia says. "He puts his feelings into them."

"He puts his hair into them," George says.

Julia waves good-bye. "Night, Ivan. Night, Bob."

I press my nose against the glass and watch her walk away. All my work, all my planning, wasted.

I look at Ruby, sleeping soundly, and suddenly I know she'll never leave the Big Top Mall. She'll be here forever, just like Stella.

I can't let Ruby be another One and Only.

chest-beating

Often, when visitors come to see me, they beat their hands against their puny chests, pretending to be me.

They pound away, soundless as the wet wings of a new butterfly.

The chest beating of a mad gorilla is not something you ever want to hear. Not even if you're wearing earplugs.

Not even if you're three miles away, wearing earplugs.

A real chest beating sends the whole jungle running, as if the sky has broken open, as if men with guns are near.

angry

Thump.

The sound—my sound—echoes through the mall.

George and Julia spin around.

Julia drops her backpack. George drops his keys. The pile of pictures goes flying.

Thump. Thump. Thump.

I bounce off the walls. I screech and bellow. I beat and beat and beat my chest.

Bob hides under Not-Tag, his paws over his ears.

I'm angry, at last.

I have someone to protect.

puzzle pieces

After a long while, I grow quiet. I sit. It's hard work, being angry.

Julia looks at me with wide, disbelieving eyes.

I'm panting. I'm a little out of shape.

"What the heck was that?" George demands.

"Something's really wrong," Julia says. "I've never seen Ivan act this way."

"He seems to be calming down, thank goodness," George says.

Julia shakes her head. "He's still upset, Dad. Look at his eyes."

My pictures are scattered all over the floor like

huge autumn leaves.

"What a mess," George says, sighing. "Wish I hadn't bothered sweeping tonight."

"Do you think Ivan's okay?" Julia asks.

"Probably just a temper tantrum," George says. He reaches under a chair to retrieve a brown and red picture. "Can't say I blame the guy, stuck in that tiny cage all these years."

Julia starts to answer, but then she freezes. She cocks her head.

She stares at her feet, where my pictures lie in disarray.

"Dad," she whispers. "Come see this."

"I'm sure he's another Rembrandt," George says. "Let's pick these up and get going, Jules. I'm exhausted."

"Dad," she says again. "Seriously. Look at this."

George follows her gaze. "I see blobs. Many, many blobs, along with the occasional swirl. Please, can we go home now?"

"That's an *H*, Dad." Julia kneels down, straightening one picture, then another. "That's an *H*, and here"—she grabs more pictures—"put this one here, and, I don't know, maybe that one. You have an *E*."

George rubs his eyes. I hold my breath.

Julia is running now. She picks up one picture, sets down another. "It's like a puzzle, Dad! This is *something*. It's a word, maybe words. And a picture of something. A giant picture."

"Jules," George says, "this is crazy." But he's looking at the floor too, wandering from picture to picture and scratching his head.

"H," Julia says. *"E. O."*

"Hoe?"

Julia chews her lower lip. *"H, E, O.* And that looks a lot like an eye."

"H, E, O, I." George writes in the air with his finger. *"I, E, O, H."*

"Not the letter. An actual eye. And that's a foot. Or maybe a tree. And a trunk. Dad, I think that's a trunk!"

Julia runs to my window. "Ivan," she whispers, "what did you make?"

I stare back. I cross my arms.

This is taking much longer than I'd thought it would.

Humans.

Sometimes they make chimps look smart.

finally

Julia and George take the pictures to the ring, where there's room to see them all.

An hour passes as they try to assemble my puzzle. Ruby's awake now, and she and Bob and I watch.

"Ivan," Ruby says, "is that a picture of me?"

"Yes," I say proudly.

"Where am I supposed to be?"

"That's a zoo, Ruby. See the walls and the grass and the people looking at you?"

Ruby squints. "Who are all those other elephants?"

"You haven't met them," I say. "Yet."

"It's a very nice zoo," Ruby says with an approving nod.

Bob nudges me with his cold nose. "It is indeed."

In the ring, Julia pumps her fist in the air. "Yes!" she cries. "I told you, Dad! There it is: H-O-M-E. *Home.*"

George gazes at the letters. He spins around to look at me. "Maybe it's just a coincidence, Jules. You know, a once-in-a-trillion kind of thing, like that old saying about the chimp and the typewriter. Give him long enough and he'll write a novel."

I make a grumbling noise. As if a chimp could write a letter, let alone a book.

"Then how do you explain the rest of it?" Julia demands. "The picture of Ruby in the zoo?"

"How do you know it's a zoo?" George asks.

"See the circle on the gate? There's a red giraffe in it."

George squints and tilts his head. "Are you sure that's a giraffe? I was thinking more along the lines of a deformed cat."

"It's the logo for the zoo, Dad. It's on all their signs. Explain that."

George gives her a helpless smile. "I can't. I can't begin to. I'm just saying there has to be a logical explanation."

"Look how big this is." Julia puts the last piece of Ruby's right ear into place. "It's huge."

"It is definitely large," George agrees.

Julia watches me. She chews on her thumbnail. I see the question in her eyes.

She turns back to the paintings and stares at them, looking, truly looking.

A slow smile dawns on Julia's face.

"Dad," she says, "I have an idea. A big idea." Julia races around the edge of my painting, her arms spread wide. "*Billboard* big."

"I'm not following you."

"I think this is meant to be on a billboard. That's what Ivan wants."

George crosses his arms over his chest. "What Ivan wants," he repeats slowly. "And you know this because . . . you two have been chatting?"

"Because I'm an artist, and he's an artist."

"Uh-huh," says George.

Julia clasps her hands together. "Come on, Dad. I'm begging you."

George shakes his head. "No. I'm not doing that. No billboard, no way."

"I'll get the ladder," Julia says. "You get the glue. I know it's dark out, but the billboard's lit."

"Mack'll fire me, Jules."

Julia considers. "But think of the publicity, Dad! Everybody would know about Ruby."

"You want me to put up a sign that shows Ruby in a zoo with the word *home* on it in giant letters?" George gestures toward my pictures. "A sign, incidentally, that just happens to have been made by a *gorilla*?"

"Exactly."

"And you want me to do it without Mack's permission?" George asks.

"Exactly."

"No," George says. "No way."

Julia goes to the edge of the ring, careful not to step on

any of my paintings. She picks up Mack's claw-stick. She walks back and hands it to her father.

George runs a finger along the blade.

"She's just a baby, Dad. Don't you want to help her?"

"But how would it help, Jules? Even if lots of people see Ivan's sign, it doesn't mean anything's going to change."

"I'm not exactly sure yet." Julia shakes her head. "Maybe people will see the sign, and they'll know this isn't where Ruby belongs. Maybe they'll want to help too."

George sighs. He looks at Ruby. She waves her trunk.

"It's a matter of principle, Dad. P-R-I-N-C-I-P-A-L."

"L-E," George corrects.

"Dad," Julia says softly, "what if Ruby ends up like Stella?"

George looks at me, at Ruby, at Julia.

He drops the claw-stick.

"The ladder," he says quietly, "is in the storage locker."

the next morning

I watch Mack's car slam to a halt in the parking lot.

He leaps out. He stares at the billboard. His jaw is open. He doesn't move for a long time.

mad human

A mad gorilla is loud. But a mad human can be loud too.

Especially when he is throwing chairs and turning over tables and breaking the cotton-candy machine.

phone call

Mack is kicking a trash can across the food court when the phone rings.

He answers it, red-faced and sweating.

"What the—" he demands.

He glares at me.

"I don't know what you're—" he starts to say, but then he stops to listen.

"Who? Julia who?" he asks. "Oh, sure. George's kid. *She's* the one who called you?"

More talking. With the phone to his ear, Mack comes closer to my cage, eyeing me suspiciously.

"Yeah, yeah," he says. "He paints. Sure. We've been

223

selling his art for quite a while now."

There is another long pause. "Yeah. Absolutely. It was my idea."

Mack nods. A smile starts at the corners of his mouth.

"Photos? No problem. You want to see him in action? Come on down, have a look. We're open 365 days a year. Can't miss us. We're right off I-95."

Mack picks up the overturned trash can. "Yeah, I think he'll be adding more pictures. It's a, you know, what do you call it? A work in progress."

When the call is done, Mack shakes his head. "Impossible," he says.

An hour later, a man with a camera comes to take my picture. He is from the local paper, the one Julia called.

"How about you take one of me with the elephant?"

Mack suggests. He drapes his arm around Ruby's back, grinning as the camera clicks.

"Perfect," the man says.

"Perfect," Mack agrees.

a star again

A photo of my billboard is in the newspaper. Mack tapes the story onto my window.

Each day more curious people arrive. They park in front of the billboard. They point and shake their heads. They take photos.

Then they come into the mall and buy my paintings.

While visitors watch, I dip my hands in fresh buckets of paint. I make pictures for the gift shop, and pictures to add to the billboard. Trees with birds. A newborn elephant with glittering black eyes. A squirrel, a bluebird, a worm.

I even paint Bob so he can be on the billboard too. I can tell he likes the picture, although he says I didn't quite capture his distinguished nose.

Every afternoon, Mack and George add my new pictures to the billboard. People slow their cars while they work. Drivers honk and wave.

My gift-shop pictures now cost sixty-five dollars (with frame).

the ape artist

I have new names. People call me the Ape Artist. The Primate Picasso.

I have visitors from morning till night, and so does Ruby.

But nothing's changed for her. Every day at two, four, and seven, Ruby plods through the sawdust with Snickers on her back.

Every night she has bad dreams.

"Bob," I say, after I've soothed Ruby to sleep with a story, "my idea isn't working."

Bob opens one eye. "Be patient."

"I'm tired of being patient," I say.

This evening a man and woman come to interview Mack and also George and Julia.

The man has a large and heavy camera perched on his shoulder. He films me as I make my pictures. He films Ruby in her cage, with her foot roped to the bolt in the floor.

"Mind if I take a look around?" he asks.

Mack waves a hand. "Be my guest."

While Mack and the woman talk, the cameraman walks through the mall. He pans his camera right and left, up and down.

When his eyes fall on the claw-stick, he stops. He trains his camera on the gleaming blade. Then he moves on.

the early news

Mack turns on the TV.

We are on *The Early News at Five O'Clock.*

Bob says don't let it go to my head.

There we all are. Mack, Ruby, me. George and Julia.
The billboard, the mall, the ring.

And the claw-stick.

signs on sticks

In the morning, several people gather in the parking lot. They're carrying signs on sticks.

The signs have words and pictures on them. One has a drawing of a gorilla cradling a baby elephant.

I wish I could read.

More people with signs come today. They want Ruby
to be free. Some of them even want Mack to shut down
the mall.

In the evening, George and Mack talk about them. Mack says they're protesting the wrong guy. He says they're going to ruin everything. He says thanks for nothing, George.

Mack stomps off. George, holding his mop, watches him leave. He rubs his eyes. He looks worried.

"Dad," Julia says, looking up from her homework. "You know what my favorite sign was?"

"Hmm?" George asks. "Which one?"

"The one that said 'Elephants Are People Too.'"

George gives her a tired smile.

He goes back to work. His mop moves across the empty food court like a giant brush, painting a picture no one will ever see.

check marks

A tall man with a clipboard and pencil comes to visit. He says he is here to inspect the property.

He doesn't say much more, but he makes many check marks on his paper.

He looks at my floor. Check. He examines Ruby's hay. Check. He eyes our water bowls. Check.

Mack watches him, scowling.

Bob is outside, hiding near the Dumpster. He does not want to be a check mark.

free ruby

Every day there are more protesters, and cameras with bright lights. Sometimes the people carrying signs shout, "Free Ruby! Free Ruby!"

"Ivan," Ruby asks, "why are those people yelling my name? Are they mad at me?"

"They're mad," I say, "but not at you."

A week later, the inspecting man comes back with a friend, a woman with smart, dark eyes like my mother's. She has a white coat on, and she smells like lobelia blossoms. Her hair is thick and brown, the color of a rotten branch teeming with luscious ants.

She watches me for a long time. Then she watches Ruby.

She talks to the man. They both talk to Mack. The

man gives Mack a sheet of paper.

Mack covers his face.

He goes to his office and slams the door.

new box

Something strange is happening. The white-coated woman is back with other humans.

They place a large box in the center of the ring.

It's Ruby sized.

And suddenly I know why the woman is here. She's here to take Ruby away.

training

The woman leads Ruby to the box. She places an apple inside. "Good girl, Ruby," she says kindly. "Don't be afraid."

Ruby inspects the box with her trunk. The woman makes a clicking sound with a little piece of metal she is holding in her hand. She gives Ruby a piece of carrot.

Each time Ruby touches the box, she gets a click and a treat.

"Why is she making that clicking noise?" I ask Bob.

"They do that to dogs all the time," Bob says. I can tell he doesn't approve. "It's called clicker training. They want Ruby to associate the noise with the treat. When she does something they want, they make that noise."

"Great job, Ruby," the woman says. "You're a quick study."

After many clicks and carrots, she takes Ruby back to her cage.

"Why is that lady giving me carrots when I touch the box?" Ruby asks me.

"I think she wants you to go inside," I explain.

"But there's nothing inside," Ruby says, "except an apple."

"Inside that box," I say, "is the way out."

Ruby tilts her head. "I don't get it."

"See the picture of the red giraffe on the box? I think the lady is from the zoo, Ruby. I think she's getting ready to take you there."

I wait for Ruby to trumpet with joy, but instead she

just stares at the box in silence.

"I'm not sure you understand. That box might be taking you to a place where there are other elephants," I say. "A place with more room, and humans who care about you."

But even as I say these words, I remember with a shudder the last box I was in.

"I don't want a zoo," Ruby says. "I want you and Bob and Julia. This is my home."

"No, Ruby," I say. "This is your prison."

poking and prodding

The lady comes again. She brings an animal doctor with an awful smell and a dangerous-looking bag.

He spends an hour with Ruby, poking and prodding. He looks at her eyes, her feet, her trunk.

When he's done with Ruby, he enters my cage. I wish I could hide under Not-Tag like Bob.

Instead I do a nice, loud chest beat, and after a moment the doctor retreats.

"We're going to need to put this one under," he says.

I'm not quite sure what he means. But I strut around my cage feeling victorious anyway.

no painting

No one asks me to paint today. No one asks Ruby to perform.

There are no shows. No visitors, unless you count the protesters.

Mack stays in his office all day.

more boxes

I wake up from a long morning nap. Bob is on my belly, but he isn't asleep. He's watching the ring, where four men are placing a large metal box.

It's me sized.

"What's that?" I ask, still blurry from sleep.

Bob nuzzles my chin. "I believe that box is for you, my friend."

I'm not sure what he means. "Me?"

"They brought in a bunch of boxes while you were sleeping. Looks to me like they're taking the whole lot of you," he says casually, licking a paw. "Even Thelma."

"Taking?" I repeat. "Taking us where?"

"Well, some to the zoo, probably. Others to an animal shelter where humans will try to find them homes." Bob shakes himself. "So. I guess all good things must come to an end, huh?"

His voice is bright, but his eyes are faraway and sad. "I'm going to miss your stomach, big guy."

Bob shuts his eyes. He makes an odd noise in his throat.

"But . . . what about you?" I ask.

I can't tell if Bob's just pretending to sleep, but he doesn't answer.

I gaze at the huge, shadowy box, and suddenly I understand how Ruby feels. I don't want to go into that box.

The last time I was in a box, my sister died.

good-bye

When George and Julia come that night, George doesn't get his mop or his broom. He gathers up his tools and belongings while Julia runs to my cage.

"This is my last night, Ivan," she says, and she presses her palm to my glass. "Mack fired my dad." Tears slip down her cheeks. "But the zoo lady said maybe they'll have an opening there in a while, cleaning cages and stuff."

I walk to the glass that separates us. I put my hand where Julia's is, palm to palm, finger to finger. My hand is bigger, but they're not so very different.

"I'm going to miss you," Julia says. "And Ruby and Bob. But this is a good thing, really it is. You deserve a different life."

I stare into her dark eyes and wish I had words for her.

Sniffling, she goes to Ruby's cage. "Have a good life, Ruby," she says.

Ruby makes a little rumbling sound. She puts her trunk between the bars and touches Julia's shoulder.

"Where is Bob, anyway?" Julia asks. She looks around, under tables, in my cage, by the trash can. "Dad," she calls, "have you seen Bob?"

"Bob? Nope," George says.

Julia's brow wrinkles. "What's going to happen to him, Dad? What if Mack shuts down the whole mall?"

"He says he's going to try to keep it open without the animals," George says. He stuffs his hands in his pockets. "I'm worried about Bob too. But he's a survivor."

"You know what, Dad?" Julia gets a gleam in her eye.

"Bob could live with us. Mom loves dogs, and he could keep her company, and—"

"Jules, I'm not even sure I have a job yet. I may not even be able to feed you, let alone some mutt."

"My dog-walking money—"

"Sorry, Jules."

Julia nods. "I understand."

She starts to leave, then runs back to my cage. "I almost forgot. This is for you, Ivan."

She slips a piece of paper into my cage. It's a drawing of Ruby and me.

We're eating yogurt raisins. Ruby is playing with another baby elephant, and I'm holding hands with a lovely gorilla.

She has red lips and a flower in her hair.

I look, as I always do in Julia's pictures, like an elegant fellow, but something is different about this drawing.

In this picture, I am smiling.

click

The door to my cage is propped open. I can't stop staring at it.

My door. Open.

The giant box has been moved, and it's open too. The humans have pushed it up against my doorway.

If I walk through my door, I enter their box.

The zoo lady, whose name is Maya, is here again.

Click. Yogurt raisin.

Click. Tiny marshmallow.

Click. Ripe papaya.

Click. Apple slice.

Hour after hour, click after click.

I look over at Ruby. She waits to see what I will do.

I touch the box.

I sniff the dark interior, where a ripe mango awaits.

Click, click, click.

I have to do it. Ruby is watching me from between the bars of her cage, and this box is the way out.

I step inside.

an idea

After I leave the box and step back into my cage, I get an idea, a good one.

I tell Bob he can sneak into my box with me and live at the zoo.

"Have you forgotten? I'm a wild beast, Ivan," he says, sniffing the floor for crumbs. "I am untamed, undaunted."

Bob samples a piece of celery and spits it out. "Besides, they'd notice. Humans are dumb, but they're not that dumb."

"Ivan?" Ruby says. "Do you think the other elephants will like me?"

"I think they'll love you, Ruby. You'll be part of their family."

"Do you think the other gorillas will like you?" Ruby asks.

"I'm a silverback, Ruby. A leader." I pull back my shoulders and hold my head high. "They don't have to like me. They have to respect me."

Even as I tell her this, I wonder if I can ever command their respect.

I haven't had much practice being a real gorilla, much less a silverback.

"Do you think the other elephants will know any jokes?"

"If they don't," I tell her, "you can teach them."

Ruby flaps her ears. She flicks her tail. "You know what, Ivan?"

"What?" I ask.

"I think I'm going to go in the box tomorrow."

I gaze at her fondly. "I think that's a good idea. And I think Stella would have agreed."

"Do you think the other elephants will know how to play tag? I love tag."

"Me too," I say, and I think of my nimble sister racing through the brush, always just out of my reach.

photo

Late at night, Mack opens my cage. The full moon falls on his sagging shoulders. He seems smaller somehow.

Bob, instantly alert, leaps off my stomach and dives under Not-Tag.

"Don't bother hiding, dog," Mack says. "I know you sleep in here." Mack settles onto my tire swing. "Might as well stay one more night. Your buddy's leaving tomorrow."

Tomorrow? My stomach drops. I'm not ready. I need more time. I haven't said my good-byes. I haven't thought this through.

Mack pulls a small photo out of his shirt pocket. It's me when I was young. Mack and I are in the front seat of his convertible.

I'm wearing a baseball cap and eating an ice cream cone.

I was a handsome lad, but I have to admit I look ridiculous. Nothing like a real gorilla.

"We had some laughs, didn't we, guy?" Mack says. "Remember when we went on that roller coaster? Or that time I tried to teach you to play basketball?" Mack shakes his head, chuckling. "You had a lousy jump shot."

He stands, sighs, looks around. He puts the photo back in his pocket.

"I'm going to miss you, Ivan," he says, and then he leaves. He doesn't look back.

leaving

Early in the morning, Maya arrives with many other humans.

Some have white coats. Some have rustling papers. They are hushed, busy, determined.

Ruby enters her box first.

"I'm scared, Ivan," she calls from inside the box. "I don't want to leave you."

A part of me doesn't want her to leave either, but I know I can't tell her that.

"Think of all the amazing stories you can share with your new family," I say.

Ruby falls silent.

"I'll tell them your elephant joke," she says after a long pause. "The one about the refrigerator."

"I bet they'd like that. And be sure to tell them about Bob and Julia and me." I clear my throat. "And Stella."

"I'll remember everyone," Ruby says. "Especially you."

Before I can say any more, they roll her cage out to a waiting truck.

It's my turn.

Bob is hiding in a corner, behind my pool. The humans don't even notice him.

While they're busy making sure my box is ready, Bob sneaks over. He licks my chin, just in case there are any leftovers.

"You," I whisper, "are the One and Only Bob."

I reach for Not-Tag. She is a limp rag without her

stuffing. Dribbles of paint cover her fur.

I hold her out to Bob. He tilts his head, confused.

"To help you sleep," I say.

Bob takes her in his teeth and slips away.

good boy

"Good Ivan, good boy," Maya says when I lumber into my box. I hear the clicker, and I'm rewarded with a tiny marshmallow.

When I'm settled, Maya gives me a sweet drink that tastes of mango and something bitter.

My eyelids grow heavy. I want to see what happens next, but I am sleepy, so sleepy.

I dream I'm with Tag and we're swinging from vines while Stella watches. The sun slices through the thick ceiling of trees and the breeze tastes like fruit.

moving

My eyes flutter open.

The box is moving.

I am in the grumbling belly of some great beast.

I fall back asleep.

awakening

I awake to glass and steel. It's a new cage not unlike my old cage, except that it's much cleaner.

Maya's here, and other humans I recognize.

"Hey there, Ivan," Maya says. "He's coming to, guys."

I have three walls of glass. The fourth wall is a curtain of wooden slats strung together.

This doesn't look like the zoos on TV. Where are the other animals?

Where are the gorillas?

Is this where Ruby ended up? In a cage just like her old cage, still alone? Is she cold? Hungry? Sad?

Is there anyone to tell her stories when she can't get to sleep?

missing

I miss my old cozy cage.

I miss my art.

But most of all, I miss Bob.

My belly's cold without him.

food

The food is fine here.

No soda, though, or cotton candy.

not famous

I have no visitors here, no sticky-fingered children or weary parents.

Only Maya and her humans come, with their soothing voices and soft hands.

I wonder if I have stopped being famous.

something in the air

Endless days pass, and then I notice something.

A change.

I don't know what it is, but I taste it in the air, like far-off rain clouds gathering.

a new tv

Maya brings me a TV. It is bigger than my old one.

She turns it on. "I think you're going to like this show," she says, smiling.

I'm hoping for a romance, or maybe a Western.

But it's a nature show, one without human voices or ads. It's a show about gorillas being gorillas. I watch them eat and groom and play-fight. I even watch them sleep.

I wonder why Mack never put on this channel.

the family

Every day I watch the gorillas on the TV screen. It's a small family and an odd one, just three females and a juvenile male, without a silverback to protect them.

They groom each other and eat and sleep, then groom each other some more. They are a contented group, placid and good-natured, although, like any family, they bicker from time to time.

excited

This morning, for some reason, there is no gorilla show
on TV.

Maya and the other humans are excited. They chirp
like birds at dawn.

"Today's the day," they say.

I've watched many humans watch me, but never have
they looked so happy.

Maya goes to the wall of wooden slats.

She grins goofily.

She pulls a string.

what I see

Gorillas.

Three females and a juvenile male.

It's the family I've been watching. But they're not on a TV screen.

They're on the other side of the glass, watching me watching them.

I see me.

Lots of me.

still there

I cover my eyes.

I look again.

They are still there.

watching

Every day, I watch them through my window, the way my visitors used to watch me.

See how they chase, groom? See how they play, sleep? See how they live?

They're graceful the way Stella was, moving just enough, only as much as they need.

They stare at me, heads tilted, pointing and hooting, and I wonder: Are they as fascinated by me as I am by them?

she

Her hoots make my ears hurt.

I admire her intact canines from afar.

Her name is Kinyani.

She is faster than I am, spry and probably smarter, although I am twice her size and that, too, is important.

She is terrifying.

And beautiful, like a painting that moves.

door

Today the humans lead me to a door.

On the other side, Kinyani and the others wait for me.

I'm not ready for this. I'm not ready to be a silverback.

I'm Ivan, just Ivan, only Ivan.

I decide it's not a good day to socialize.

I'll try again tomorrow.

wondering

All night I lie awake, wondering about Ruby.

Has she already walked through a door like the one I'm facing?

Was she as scared as I am? Scared the way she must have been that day she fell in the hole?

I think of Ruby's endless curiosity, and of the questions she loved to ask. *Have you ever danced with a tiger, Ivan? Will your fur turn blue? Why doesn't that little boy have a tail?*

If Ruby were here with me, she'd be asking: *What's on the other side of the door, Ivan?*

Ruby would want to know, and she would have been through that door by now.

ready

"Want to try again, Ivan?" Maya asks. I think of Ruby, and I tell myself it's time.

The door opens.

outside at last

Sky.
Grass.
Tree.
Ant.
Stick.
Bird.
Dirt.
Cloud.
Wind.
Flower.
Rock.
Rain.

Mine.
Mine.
Mine.

oops

I sniff, approach, strut a bit, but the others don't welcome me. They have sharp teeth and loud voices.

Did I do something wrong?

Kinyani chases me. She throws a stick at me. She corners me.

I know that she's testing me to see if I'm a true silverback, one who can protect her family.

I cower and hide my eyes.

Maya lets me back into my cage.

what it was like

I lie awake and try to remember what it was like, being a gorilla.

How did we move? How did we touch? How did we know who was boss?

I try to think past the babies and the motorbikes and the popcorn and the short pants.

I try to imagine Ivan as he might have been.

pretending

The juvenile male approaches. He's eyeing my food hungrily.

I imagine a different Ivan, my father's son.

I grumble and swat and swagger. I beat my chest till the whole world hears.

Kinyani watches, and so do the others.

I move toward the young upstart, and he retreats.

Almost as if he believes I'm the silverback I'm pretending to be.

nest

I'm making a nest on the ground. It isn't a true jungle nest. The leaves are inferior and the sticks are brittle. They snap when I weave them into place.

The others watch, grunting their disapproval: *too small, too flimsy, an ugly thing to see.*

But when I climb into that leafy cradle, it's like floating on treetop mist.

Maya wants me to go back to my glass cage. I can tell, because she is tempting me toward the door with a trail of tiny marshmallows.

I try to ignore her. I don't want to leave the outside. It's a cloudless day, and I've found just the right spot for a nap. But I relent when she adds yogurt raisins to the trail. She knows my weaknesses all too well.

In the glass cage, the TV is on. It's another nature show, jerky and unfocused.

I expect to see gorillas, but none appear.

I hear a shrill sound, like a toy trumpet.

My heart quickens.

I rush close to the screen, and there she is.

Ruby.

She is rolling in a lovely pool of mud with two other young elephants.

Another elephant approaches. She towers over Ruby. She strokes Ruby, nudges her. She makes soft noises.

They stand side by side, just the way Stella and Ruby used to do. Their trunks entwine. I see something new in Ruby's eyes, and I know what it is.

It's joy.

I watch the whole thing, and then Maya plays it again for me, and again. At last she turns off the TV and carries it out of the cage.

I put my hand to the glass. Maya looks over.

Thank you, I try to say with my eyes. Thank you.

it

Kinyani ambles toward me. She taps me on the shoulder and knuckle runs away.

I watch her, arms crossed over my chest. I'm careful not to make a sound.

I'm not sure what we're doing.

She ambles back, shoves at me, dashes past. And then I realize what's happening.

We're playing.

We're playing *tag*.

And I'm it.

romance

Make eye contact.

Show your form.

Strut.

Grunt.

Throw a stick.

Grunt some more.

Make some moves.

Romance is hard work.

It looks so easy on TV.

I'm not sure I will ever get the hang of it.

I wish Bob were here. I could use some advice.

I try to recall all the romance movies we watched together.

I remember the talking, the hugging, the face licking.

I'm not very good at this.

But it's fun trying.

grooming

Is there anything sweeter than the touch of another as she pulls a dead bug from your fur?

talk

Gorillas aren't chatty, like humans, prone to gossip and bad jokes.

But now and again we swap a story under the sun.

One day it's my turn.

I tell my troop about Mack and Ruby and Bob and Stella and Julia and George, about my mother and father and sister.

When I am done, they look away, silent.

Kinyani moves closer. Her shoulder brushes mine, and we let the sun soak into our fur. Together.

I've explored every nook and cranny of this place, except for a hill at the far end where workers have been repairing a wall.

They're finally gone. They've left behind fresh white brick and a mound of black dirt.

While the others laze in the morning sun, I want to explore the hilltop. They've been there before, and I have not. Everything is still fresh to my eyes.

I take my time going uphill, savoring the feel of grass on my knuckles. The breeze carries the shouts of children and the drowsy hum of bumblebees. Near the top of the hill is a low-limbed tree, the kind my sister would have loved.

The wall is endless, clean and white, stretching far down to the habitats beyond my own. It's high and wide, carefully built to keep us in and others out.

This is, after all, still a cage.

It rained last night, and the pile of dirt is soft to the touch. I scoop up a handful and breathe in the loamy smell.

It's a rich brown color, heavy and cool in my palm.

And the wall waits, like an endless blank billboard.

the wall

It's a big wall.

But it's a big pile of dirt, and I'm a big artist.

I slap handfuls of mud on the warm cement. I make a handprint.

I tap my nose with a muddy finger. I make a noseprint.

I slide my palms up and down. The mud is thick and hard to use. But I keep moving and scooping and spreading.

I don't know what I'm making, and I don't care. I make swoops and swirls and thick lines. Figures and shapes. Light and shadow.

I'm an artist at work.

When I'm done, I step back to admire my work. But it's a large canvas, and I'd like to get a better view.

I go to the thick-limbed tree and grab the lowest branch. I try to swing my legs.

Umph. I land hard. I'm too big to climb, I suppose.

I try again anyway, and this time I pull myself onto the first limb, gasping for breath.

One more limb, two, and I can't go any farther. Perched halfway up the tree, I see my troop, still dozing contentedly.

I take in the wall, splattered and splashed with mud. Not much color, but lots of movement. I like it. It feels dreamy and wild, like something Julia might have made.

From my seat in the tree, I can see beyond the wall. I

see giraffes and hippos. I see deer with legs like delicate twigs. I see a bear snoozing in a hollow log.

I see elephants.

She's far away, belly deep in tall grass with others by her side.

Ruby.

"She's here, Stella," I whisper. "Ruby's safe. Just like I promised."

I call to Ruby, but the wind tugs at my words and I know she'll never hear me.

Still, Ruby pauses for a second, her ears spread wide like tiny sails.

Then, with lumbering grace, she moves on through the grass.

silverback

It's a cloudy evening, chill and drizzly. Dinner is on its way, but I don't care.

At night we sleep in our den, but I'm always the last to head inside. I've been inside long enough.

This time of day, there aren't many visitors. Just a few stragglers, leaning on the wall that separates us. They point, take a couple photos, then head over to the nearby giraffes.

One of the keepers is beckoning. Reluctantly I turn to go.

Out of the corner of my eye, I see someone running. I pause.

It's a girl with dark hair, lugging a backpack. A man

follows behind, racing to catch up.

"Ivan!" the girl yells. "Ivan!"

It's Julia!

I scramble to the edge of the wide moat that skirts the wall.

Julia and George wave to me. I dash back and forth, hooting and grunting, doing a gorilla dance of happiness.

"Calm down," says a voice. "You're behaving like a chimp."

I freeze.

A tiny, nut-brown, big-eared head pops out of Julia's backpack.

"Nice place," Bob says.

"Bob," I say. "It's really you."

"In the flesh."

"How . . . where . . ." I can't seem to find any words.

"George's job at the zoo doesn't start till next month, so he and Julia made an agreement. She's walking three extra dogs to cover my food. And get this: they're *all poodles.*"

"You said you didn't want a home," I say.

"Yeah," Bob says. "But Julia's mom likes my company. So I figure I'm doing everybody a favor. It's a win-win."

Julia pushes Bob's head back inside her backpack. "You're not supposed to be here," she reminds him.

"Ivan looks great, doesn't he, Jules?" George asks. "Stronger. Happier, even."

Julia holds up a little photo, but it's too far away for me to see. "It's Ruby, Ivan. She's with other elephants now. Because of you."

I know, I want to tell her. I saw with my own eyes.

We stare across the expanse that separates us. After a while, George pats Julia's arm. "Time to go, Jules."

Julia gives a wistful smile. "Bye, Ivan. Say hello to your new family." She turns to George. "Thank you, Dad."

"For what?"

"For—" She gestures toward me. "For this."

They turn to leave. The lamps that light the zoo pathways blink on, blanketing the world with yellow light.

I can just make out Bob's little head sticking out of Julia's backpack. "You are the One and Only Ivan," he calls.

I nod, then turn toward my family, my life, my home.

"Mighty Silverback," I whisper.

acknowledgments

My thanks to the talented folks at HarperCollins for their expertise and enthusiasm. A special shout-out to art director extraordinaire, Amy Ryan; to the incomparable Sarah Hoy for her lovely book design; and to copyeditor Renée Cafiero, the best in the biz.

Most of all, I'm indebted to Anne Hoppe, my remarkable editor, who has the ear of a poet, the eye of an artist, and the patience of a preschool teacher (and those are just a few of her superpowers). Thank you, Anne, for everything. I couldn't have done this without you. Really.

To my parents, Roger and Suzanne; my siblings, Stu, Martha, and Lisa; my dear, old (but not *that* old!) friends Lisa Leach and Suzanne Hultman: I know how truly lucky I am to have you in my life.

And to Julia, Jake, and Michael: Humans have so many words, more than we truly need. Still, there are no words that can ever express how much I love you all.

BONUS MATERIAL

Read on for a special look at the sequel to
The One and Only Ivan, *starring Bob*

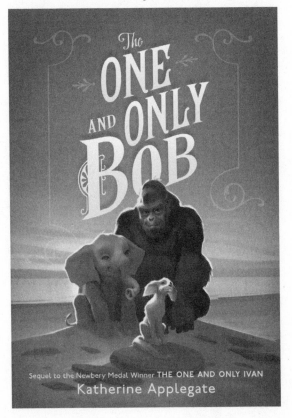

let's play

life's good

get lost

I'm scared

I'm cool

I surrender

canine glossary

bed boogie: circular "dance" performed by dogs
before settling into bed, probably a primitive nesting
behavior

copilot: dog riding in car, often with head poking out
of an open window (*see also:* drool flag)

crazy mutt: exuberant greeting ritual

drool flag: visible tongue protrusion, frequently
displayed during copiloting or meal preparation

FRAP: frenetic random activity period (*synonym:*
zoomies)

full wag: the happiest tail position, a relaxed circular
swish, sometimes including hip wiggles

fur on alert: raised hair on a dog's neck and back, an involuntary reaction often caused by fright or aggression

head tilt: quizzical look employed to charm gullible humans

LEAVE IT: the world's worst command, especially when applied to food

me-ball: dried excrement thrown at observers (*origin: Gorilla, informal*)

playbow: body position with elbows down and rear up, signaling an invitation to have fun

rhymes-with-pet-threat: vet, an otherwise kind human armed with thermometers and needles

tailspin: (I) chase involving the flexible appendage attached to the rear of most canines; (2) (*informal*) an embarrassing or quixotic effort

toe-twitcher: dream (often squirrel-focused) resulting in foot movement

tug-of-war string: a long (though never long enough) piece of fabric or leather used to lead humans during walks

UFO: (I) unidentified food object, often found under kitchen tables or couch cushions; (2) unidentified floor object, hopefully edible; (3) unidentified flying object, ideally a stick, flying disk, or slobber-covered tennis ball

water bowl of power: (I) jumbo-sized ceramic dish; (2) uncomfortable human chair, generally found in bathrooms

zoomies: sudden bursts of energy, usually involving chaotic dashes through the house (*informal; see also:* FRAP)

confession

Look, nobody's ever accused me of being a good dog.

I bark at empty air. I eat cat litter. I roll in garbage to enhance my aroma.

I harass innocent squirrels. I hog the couch. I lick myself in the presence of company.

I'm no saint, okay?

and while i'm at it . . .

I may or may not have eaten a pepperoni pizza with anchovies when nobody was looking.

Also, I may or may not have eaten a coconut vanilla birthday cake when nobody was looking.

Also, I may or may not have eaten a Thanksgiving turkey (except for the stuffing—*way* too much rosemary) when nobody was looking.

Nobody looking. That seems to be the common thread.

As they say on the crime shows: motive and opportunity.

robert

Name's Bob.

I'm a mutt of uncertain heritage. Definitely some Chihuahua, with a smidgen of papillon on my father's side.

You're probably thinking I'm some wimpy lap dog. The kind you see poking out of an old lady's purse like a hairy key chain. But size ain't everything.

It's swagger. Attitude. You gotta have the moves.

Probably I shoulda been named Bruiser or Bamm-Bamm or Bandit, but Bob's what I got and Bob'll do me just fine.

Julia named me. Long time ago. She's my girl. She calls me "Robert" when I get on her nerves.

Happens pretty often, to be honest.

numero uno

There's an old saying about us dogs, goes like this: *It's no coincidence that man's best friend can't talk.*

Lemme tell you something. If we *could* talk to people, they'd get an earful.

You ever hear anyone mention man being dog's best friend?

Nope?

Didn't think so.

Way I've always figured it, end of the day, you gotta be your own best friend. Look out for numero uno.

Learned that one the hard way.

That's not to say I don't have a best pal. I do.

Gorilla, name of Ivan. Big guy and I go way, way back.

Gorilla and dog. Yep, I know. You don't see that every day. Long story.

I love that big ol' ape. Ditto our little elephant friend, Ruby.

They're the best.

how we met

The first time I met Ivan, I was a homeless puppy. Desperate, starving, all alone.

It was the middle of the night, and I'd slipped into the mall where Ivan lived in a cage. I wandered a bit, grateful for the warmth, confused by the weird assortment of sleeping animals I found there, checking every trash can for anything edible.

There was a small hole in a corner of Ivan's enclosure. He was fast asleep, cuddled up with a worn stuffed animal that looked like a weary gorilla.

He was snoring, and man, that guy snored like a pro.

In his open palm was a chunk of banana, and—I still get shivers when I think about this—I ate it right out of his hand.

Guy coulda squeezed his fingers shut and I woulda popped like a puppy balloon. But he just kept on sleeping.

And then—more shivers—I am either a maniac or the bravest dog on the planet, probably a little of both—I hopped up onto that big, round, furry tummy of his.

That's right. I climbed Mount Ivan.

Crazy, I know. I have no idea what I was thinking. Maybe I was so exhausted I went a little bonkers. Maybe he just looked so warm and cozy that I figured it was worth taking a chance.

I did my bed boogie. Dogs don't feel right till we do a quick dance before settling.

Once I had things just so, I lay down in a little puppy lump and rode the waves on that tummy like a puny boat on a great brown sea.

When Ivan opened his eyes the next morning, he didn't seem surprised in the least to find a puppy snoozing on his belly. He refused to move until I woke up.

I think he was as glad as I was to have found a new friend.

Author's Note

The *One and Only Ivan* is a work of fiction, but the inspiration for this imagined tale lies in a true story.

Ivan, a real gorilla, lived at Zoo Atlanta, but on the way to that happy ending, he spent almost three decades without seeing another of his own kind.

After being captured as an infant in what is now the Democratic Republic of the Congo (Ivan's twin sister died en route to the U.S. or shortly thereafter), Ivan was raised in a home until he became unmanageable. At that point he was added to an odd collection of animals housed at a circus-themed mall in Washington state.

Ivan spent twenty-seven years of his life alone in a cage. Over time, as an understanding of primate needs and behavior grew, public discomfort with Ivan's lonely state grew as well, particularly after he was featured in a *National Geographic* special entitled *The Urban Gorilla*. A public outcry followed, including heartfelt letters from children. When the mall where Ivan lived went bankrupt, he was placed on permanent loan to Zoo Atlanta, which houses the largest group of captive western lowland gorillas in the nation.

Ivan became a beloved celebrity at Zoo Atlanta, where he lived contentedly with Kinyani and other gorillas. He was known for his paintings, which were often "signed" with his thumbprint.

Ivan and Kinyani were real gorillas—and so, by the way, was Jambo, whose story Stella tells to Ivan and Bob. But all other characters and situations in this novel are entirely the product of my imagination. When I started to write about the grim facts of Ivan's solitary existence, a new tale slowly began to take shape. At least on the page, where anything is possible, I wanted to give Ivan (even while captive behind the walls of his tiny cage) a voice of his own and a story to tell. I wanted to give him someone to protect, and the chance to be the mighty silverback he was always meant to be.

Visit HarperCollins.com for more resources for The One and Only Ivan!

Ivan's Signature

Dear Reader,

Every summer, my friend Donna and I rely on students, teachers, librarians, and authors from around the world to help us pick a character from a children's book to take on a literary road trip. During the 2012 road trip, we traveled over 4,000 miles with a stuffed gorilla who wore a personalized T-shirt that author Katherine Applegate had specially made, and a copy of *The One and Only Ivan*.

If I asked stuffed-animal Ivan to write about the most memorable afternoon during our journey, I know he would waste few words describing when the REAL Ivan stood five feet from us and signed my copy of *The One and Only Ivan*. My eyes fill with tears just thinking about that memorable afternoon. I can still see Ivan's loving caretaker, Jodi, feeding him blueberries. I hear her say, "Ivan, are you ready to sign your book?" She gently guides his finger into a can of green paint. He presses down inside the book, leaving his distinguished mark. After he signs the book, he does not let us out of his sight—it looks as though the deepest, wisest thoughts are running through his head.

I sent Jodi the following email message on January 28, 2013, the day *The One and Only Ivan* won the Newbery Medal:

> Dear Jodi,
> "I hope *The One and Only Ivan* wins the Newbery Medal" is the last thing you said to me when I met you and Ivan. It happened! It really happened! It fills my heart with joy to know kids will always know about Ivan, the mighty silverback, who touched your heart and mine. Thank you for taking care of Ivan for so many years.
> *Best, John*

I'm so happy to be able to share Ivan's signature with you.

—John Schumacher
www.mrschureads.blogspot.com

I v:
th
A
hi
glass w
his life
thinks

Inste
seen an
elephar
Ivan th
the tas
with co

Ther
taken f
see thei
new eye
with he
change

Kath
poignar
first-pe
ship, art

KATH

The

ONE

AN

O

illustrations by
Patricia Castelao

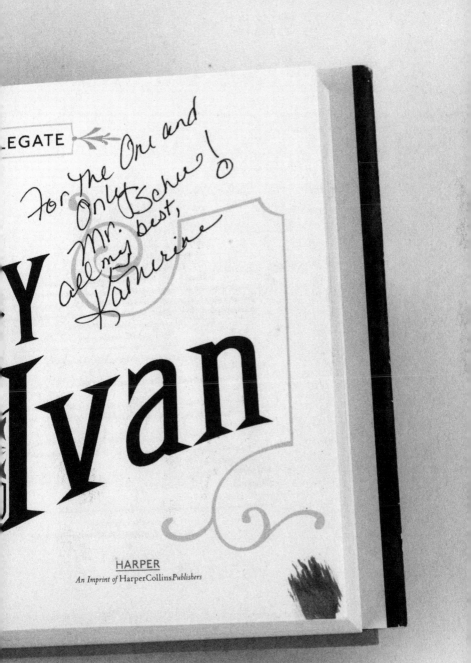

For The One and
Only Schue!
all my best,
Katherine

The Endling series by
KATHERINE APPLEGATE

When one is endangered, all are in peril!

Book One   Book Two

The last of her kind.
The first to lead a revolt.

HARPER
An Imprint of HarperCollinsPublishers

www.harpercollinschildrens.com • www.endlingbooks.com

DISNEY
The One And Only
IVAN

Turn the page for scenes from the movie
and read what the actors have to say
about the story, in their own words.

"Julia's relationship with Ivan is very special, because Julia feels very lonely sometimes and so does Ivan. Even though Ivan can't really speak to her, in his eyes he does."

Ariana Greenblatt stars as Julia, whose dad, George, works at the mall.

"Mack is a showman, and he rises to the occasion with the point of view that the show must go on."

Bryan Cranston's character, Mack, is the ringmaster of all the shows.

"Ivan's mission is that he's got
to get Ruby out of there."

Sam Rockwell voices Ivan,
the silverback gorilla.

"I genuinely love Bob, my character. And he loves Ivan because Ivan is his best friend. Plus, he has a big belly and TV—and I love sleeping on Ivan's belly, watching TV."

Danny DeVito voices Ivan's friend Bob.

"Stella sees Ivan as he is. She loves him, and she
has more faith in him than he has in himself."

Angelina Jolie voices Stella, one of Ivan's friends and the elephant who takes Ruby under her wing.

"I hope when audiences see The One and Only Ivan, they will feel what I felt, which is a sense of compassion for animals and their treatment by humans. I had a desire to understand them better and thereby understand ourselves better through them. How we treat animals is indicative of how we treat each other."

Bryan Cranston stars as Mack, who runs the Exit 8 Big Top Mall and Video Arcade.

"The story of Ivan is really about friendship.
And it's about learning that it's never
too late to find out who you really are."

Thea Sharrock is the director of the movie
The One and Only Ivan.

"No matter what your obstacles, there's always a way to work it out."

Chaka Khan voices the character of Henrietta, the chicken.

"Ruby really looks up to Stella and really adores her because she didn't have parents and now Stella's being her parent."

Brooklynn Prince voices the character of Ruby, the baby elephant.

"Ivan's getting a second chance at becoming a hero."

Sam Rockwell's character, Ivan, gets a big idea from his love of drawing.